CW00967723

THE DEAD
AND OTHER STORIES

THE DEAD
AND OTHER STORIES

James Joyce

a *Broadview Anthology of British Literature* edition

Contributing Editor, *The Dead and Other Stories*:
Melissa Free, Arizona State University

General Editors,
Broadview Anthology of British Literature:
Joseph Black, University of Massachusetts, Amherst
Leonard Conolly, Trent University
Kate Flint, University of Southern California
Isobel Grundy, University of Alberta
Don LePan, Broadview Press
Roy Liuzza, University of Tennessee
Jerome J. McGann, University of Virginia
Anne Lake Prescott, Barnard College
Barry V. Qualls, Rutgers University
Claire Waters, University of California, Davis

broadview press

© 2014 Broadview Press

All rights reserved. The use of any part of this publication reproduced, transmitted in any form or by any means, electronic, mechanical, photocopying, recording, or otherwise, or stored in a retrieval system, without prior written consent of the publisher—or in the case of photocopying, a licence from Access Copyright (Canadian Copyright Licensing Agency), One Yonge Street, Suite 1900, Toronto, Ontario M5E 1E5—is an infringement of the copyright law.

Library and Archives Canada Cataloguing in Publication

Joyce, James, 1882-1941, author
    The dead and other stories / James Joyce ; contributing editor, The dead and other stories, Melissa Free ; contributing editors, Joseph Black, Leonard Conolly, Kate Flint, Isobel Grundy, Don LePan, Roy Liuzza, Jerome J. McGann, Anne Lake Prescott, Barry V. Qualls, Claire Waters.

(Broadview anthology of British literature)
ISBN 978-1-55481-165-6 (pbk.)

    I. Free, Melissa, 1969-, contributing editor of compilation II. Black, Joseph, 1962-, editor of compilation III. Title. IV. Series: Broadview anthology of British literature

PR6019.O9D4 2014   823'.912   C2013-908202-6

Broadview Press is an independent, international publishing house, incorporated in 1985.

We welcome comments and suggestions regarding any aspect of our publications—please feel free to contact us at the addresses below or at broadview@broadviewpress.com.

North America	PO Box 1243, Peterborough, Ontario K9J 7H5, Canada 555 Riverwalk Parkway, Tonawanda, NY 14150, USA Tel: (705) 743-8990; Fax: (705) 743-8353 email: customerservice@broadviewpress.com
UK, Europe, Central Asia, *Middle East, Africa, India,* *and Southeast Asia*	Eurospan Group, 3 Henrietta St., London WC2E 8LU, UK Tel: 44 (0) 1767 604972; Fax: 44 (0) 1767 601640 email: eurospan@turpin-distribution.com
Australia and New Zealand	NewSouth Books, c/o TL Distribution 15-23 Helles Ave., Moorebank, NSW 2170, Australia Tel: (02) 8778 9999; Fax: (02) 8778 9944 email: orders@tldistribution.com.au

www.broadviewpress.com

Developmental Editors: Jennifer McCue and Laura Buzzard

Broadview Press acknowledges the financial support of the Government of Canada through the Canada Book Fund for our publishing activities.

PRINTED IN CANADA

Contents

Introduction

James Joyce and *Dubliners*

Irish novelist James Joyce's innovative prose style and choice of subject matter had an enormous influence on twentieth-century literature; as fellow writer T.S. Eliot phrased it, Joyce helped make "the modern world possible for art" by discovering "a way of controlling, or ordering, of giving a shape and a significance to the panorama of futility and anarchy which is contemporary history." Joyce's works as a whole redefined realism through their efforts to access reality as perceived by the mind—whether awake or dreaming. Although throughout his life he battled publishers, critics, and readers who objected to his frank treatment of the more "vulgar" aspects of his characters' thoughts and actions, Joyce became a literary figure of the first magnitude during his lifetime, and has remained so since.

James Augustus Aloysius Joyce, born in the middle-class Dublin suburb of Rathgar, was the first surviving son in a family of twelve siblings. Through his father's fecklessness, Joyce's family situation would eventually devolve into poverty; John Joyce's increasing dependence on alcohol created strains both on the family's finances and on its morale. On the other hand, Joyce's mother, Mary Jane Joyce, exposed the young Joyce to the arts and to religion, as she was accomplished in music and devout in her Catholicism. The former he would embrace as fervently as he would one day reject the latter.

At the age of six, Joyce started his studies under the tutorship of the Jesuits. During the course of his schooling, however, he became increasingly cynical about the Church. His intellectual and spiritual rebelliousness grew so that by the time he entered university he had begun to believe that religion, family, and nation were all traps of conventionality that the true artist must avoid.

While at University College, Dublin, Joyce wrote poetry, as well as articles that parodied various literary styles. The penchant for experimentation with form he displayed during this time stayed with him throughout his writing career, from the economy of voice exhibited in *Dubliners*, to the variety of narrative expressions created for *A Portrait of the Artist as a Young Man* and *Ulysses*, to the radical linguistic experimentation of *Finnegans Wake*. In political matters, he rejected the single-minded nationalism of his peers and wrote outspoken articles, which were published privately after the school advisory board barred their publication in the school newspaper. Meanwhile, he was very successful in his chosen field of study: modern languages.

Joyce moved to Paris in 1902 to study medicine, but it was not until 1904 that he took up his artistic mission in earnest and decided to leave Ireland for good. Deeply ambivalent about his original home, Joyce visited Ireland only twice after his 1904 emigration to Europe, though he would return again and again in the pages of his fiction. For Joyce, exile was a prerequisite for artistic objectivity and freedom; he believed that his self-imposed exile allowed him to see the truth of Ireland and Irishness with clarity, precision, and detachment.

In 1904, Joyce met the woman who would be his lifelong partner. As legend has it, it was on 16 June, or "Bloomsday" (the day on which the events in *Ulysses* take place), that Joyce first went out walking with Nora Barnacle, a chambermaid from Galway. Uninterested in literature, but with a fresh charm and wit and, like Joyce, an interest in music, she went with Joyce to the city of Pola, in the Austro-Hungarian Empire, four months after their meeting. They lived there, unmarried, for a short time, and later moved to Trieste (also part of Austro-Hungary, and then part of Italy after World War I), where Joyce continued to write while eking out a meager living teaching English. The couple had two children, Lucia and Georgio, and married in 1931.

Just a month after Joyce met Nora, he began writing the material that would eventually become *Dubliners*. While it is now one of the most admired short story collections in western literature, it was nearly a decade before Joyce succeeded in getting *Dubliners* published, a half a century before it was readily available in Ireland, and another few years before it received significant scholarly attention. It began life as follows: George Russell (better known as A.E.) solicited a story from Joyce for the *Irish Homestead*, the weekly publication of the Irish Agricultural Organization. "Could you write anything simple, rural?, livemaking?, pathos?," he inquired, "which could be inserted so as not to shock readers?"[1] Joyce immediately drafted "The Sisters," which he signed "Stephen Daedalus," the name of the protagonist of his novel-in-progress that would eventually become *A Portrait of the Artist as a Young Man* (in which Stephen's surname is spelled "Dedalus"). "Eveline" and "After the Race" soon followed "The Sisters," after which Russell, who had received numerous complaints from readers offended, if not shocked, at Joyce's representation of Dublin life, declined to accept any more. But by this point, the confident twenty-two year old had conceived of making the three stories part of a collection, which he would call *Dubliners*, and which, he wrote, would "betray the soul of that hemiplegia or paralysis which many consider a city."[2]

By early 1906, Joyce had secured a contract with the English publisher Grant Richards, who subsequently expressed concerns over words ("bloody"), passages (several in "Counterparts"), and an entire story ("Two Gallants"), which the printer had found morally objectionable—and which Richards felt the public would find morally objectionable as well. Joyce's view was that Richards was "retard[ing] the course of civilization in Ireland by preventing the Irish people from having one good look at themselves in my nicely polished looking-glass." Although he eventually made many concessions to the publisher, Richards still declined to publish the book. History would repeat itself just a few years later when Maunsel and Company, the Irish publisher with whom Joyce had signed a contract in 1909, refused to follow through, citing objections to the use of real names, an oblique reference to King Edward VII's personal life (in "Ivy Day in the Committee Room"), and the entirety of "An Encounter" (which alludes to sexual deviance). By the time that *Dubliners* was finally published in 1914—by Richards, now with a new publishing house—*Portrait* had begun to appear serially in the avant-garde journal *The Egoist*, largely eclipsing the short-story collection. *Ulysses* and *Finnegans Wake* would follow, but with the exception of *Chamber Music* (Joyce's first published book and his only collection of poetry), none of Joyce's books would be freely available throughout Ireland until after his death.

---

1 See appendices B.1 and D.3 in the "In Context" materials at the end of this volume.
2 Joyce also planned to write a companion collection to be titled *Provincials*, which sadly never materialized.

Viewed for most of the twentieth century as the quintessential cosmopolitan modernist, Joyce has only recently been read as a specifically Irish writer. Certainly, *Dubliners* (like Joyce's later works) is a modernist text. Impressionistic, ambiguous, and creatively employing free indirect discourse (a narrative style in which a third-person narrator borrows the idiom of the characters), it shows the influence of experimental writers such as Ibsen and Chekhov. Full of symbols, parallels, and repetition, Joyce's work also shows the influence of symbolists such as Arthur Symons and Yeats. At the same time, the work reflects to some extent the realist tradition of writers such as Gogol and Flaubert. *Dubliners* is doggedly specific about both place (streets, parks, monuments, hotels, and businesses) and time (the precise dates on which several of the stories take place can be readily identified); it draws on real events and people; and, with its detailed references to political, religious, and cultural life in turn-of-the-century Dublin, it functions as a kind of anthropological study of urban life.

The text is largely concerned with the many difficulties faced by Dublin's lower-middle class. The problems plaguing early twentieth-century Dublin included an economic depression, in which the country had been mired since the Great Famine (1845–52); a trend toward extremely late marriage; a limited range of opportunities available to women; widespread alcoholism; the sometimes stifling religious and social control exerted by the Catholic Church; and the oppressive colonialism of the British Empire. As the first paragraph of the first story ("The Sisters") suggests, passivity, emptiness, and corruption (signified by "*paralysis*," "*gnomon*," and "*simony*") are the most debilitating effects and responses elicited by this morass of difficulties. Joyce described *Dubliners* as "a chapter of the moral history of my country," a country that he felt had betrayed its own best interests in its blind allegiance to the Church, its rigid adherence to social mores, its cultural romanticism (as expressed, for example, in the Celtic Revival encouraged by Joyce's contemporaries such as Lady Gregory, W.B. Yeats, and J.M. Synge), and its fractious nationalism.

Conceiving of *Dubliners* as something of a bildungsroman, Joyce identified "childhood, adolescence, maturity, and public life" as four "aspects" ordering the stories. This structure becomes apparent only as one makes one's way through the collection; there is no external apparatus identifying the various sections. Nor are there any fixed links between stories; while a number of the characters from *Dubliners* appear in *Ulysses*, no character appears, or is referred to, in more than one story in *Dubliners* itself. Each story, then, can be read independently. At the same time, recurring themes, imagery, and language appear throughout, neighboring stories often speak to one another, the stories within each (unmarked) section relate to the others, and the first and last stories in the book—"The Sisters" and "The Dead"— have a number of parallels (their titles, for example, could easily be switched). There is, thus, not only a logic to the sequence of the stories but also a unity to the collection as a whole, one that is reflected in the selections made for this volume.

Despite the book's loose bildungsroman structure and its inclusion of a number of potentially epiphanic moments, many critics have questioned whether *Dubliners* suggests the possibility of growth. Indeed, a number of characters may experience an "epiphany," as Joyce put it—a flash of awareness or self-recognition—but there is never any indication that such moments of clarity necessarily compel transformation. The reader, thus, is often left wondering whether awareness is enough to produce change. What, if anything, does the boy learn in "Araby"? Does the eponymous Eveline forfeit hope or protect her future by failing, or declining, to join Frank? What do Little Chandler's "tears of remorse" signify in the curiously named "A Little Cloud"? And what is the meaning of Gabriel's vision in "The Dead"? In "betray[ing] ... the paralysis" of Dublin is Joyce merely condemning it, or is he signaling the possibility of the "spiritual liberation" toward which he claims the text is itself "the first step"?

These and other questions to which the stories' open-endedness gives rise bespeak the stories' modernist sensibility, even as their "style of scrupulous meanness," in Joyce's words, bespeaks their realism. It was Joyce's particular genius not only to convey with startling precision life in late Victorian and Edwardian Dublin, but also to make his depiction broadly accessible. A century after *Dubliners'* publication, as we face economic and social struggles at the beginning of another new century—arguably also a new era—the collection is as relevant as it ever was, its language as beautiful, its ambiguities as compelling.

The five stories included in this collection represent each of the four groupings identified by Joyce, while together covering a range of themes prominent in *Dubliners* as a whole. "The Sisters," written first and situated first, both here and in *Dubliners*, introduces readers to such themes as the pervasion of the unspoken, the mysteries of Catholicism, and the proximity of death—all through a child's eyes. "Araby," another tale of childhood, draws from the languages of romance literature and Orientalism,[1] reminding readers of Ireland's unique and ambivalent relationship to Britain (one that critic Joseph Valente has aptly termed "metrocolonial").[2] "Eveline," a story of adolescence, illustrates the challenges faced by single women and the lure of immigration. "A Little Cloud," a tale of maturity, explores homosociality, the proximity—and specter—of England, and the cultural prevalence of the Celtic Revival. "The Dead," arguably a story of public life,[3] depicts Irish "hospitality," the Irish Ireland Movement, religion, and family. Written more than a year after Joyce had finished the others, it was meant to redress what he felt was their "unnecessar[y] harsh[ness]." It is a haunting tale of connection and alienation, celebration and lamentation, the living and the dead, which reflects, in the words of Stanislaus Joyce, "the nostalgic love of a rejected exile," even as, in keeping with the rest of the collection, it undercuts it. Set on the feast of the Epiphany, it underscores one of the central themes of *Dubliners*: the dubious possibility of transformation through the self-recognition that is the heart of epiphany.

By far the longest story in the collection, "The Dead" is undoubtedly an important work in its own right. Since Thomas Loe's 1991 contention that that "*The Dead* is a novella," it has increasingly been

---

1 In *Orientalism* (1978), Edward Said described a discourse (long prevalent in Europe) that made a geographical, demographical, moral, cultural, and hierarchical distinction between the East and the West; made little if any distinction between parts of the East; and associated the East with exoticism, despotism, irrationality, and backwardness, and the West with normalcy, democracy, reason, and civilization, thereby "justifying" European imperialism.

2 The term "metrocolonial," in Valente's usage," refers to Ireland's "unique and contradictory position" as both a colony of the British Empire (since the twelfth century) and an "active constituent" at the metropolitan heart of that empire (since the formation of the United Kingdom of Great Britain and Ireland in 1801).

3 Because "The Dead" was written as an afterthought, Joyce did not list it in the four-part schema he outlined for the collection. An early version of this outline is included in the contextual materials (see Appendix B.4, Letter to Grant Richards, 5 May 1906), though it is not the one that lists the stories by name.

read as such. There is, however, no consensus on what distinguishes a novella from either a long short story or a short novel in terms of length, nor on whether the novella is a distinct form in terms of convention. For some, such as Ian McEwan, the novella has a unique capacity both to develop themes and characters in ways characteristic of the novel and to employ the intensity and compression that characterize the short story. McEwan, who is known primarily as a novelist, has also written an acclaimed novella, *On Chesil Beach* (2007). Writing about the latter genre in the *New Yorker* in 2012, he stated:

> I believe the novella is the perfect form of prose fiction. It is the beautiful daughter of a rambling, bloated ill-shaven giant (but a giant who's a genius on his best days).... [In the novella], the demands of economy push writers to polish their sentences to precision and clarity, to bring off their effects with unusual intensity, to remain focused on the point of their creation and drive it forward with functional single-mindedness, and to end it with a mind to its unity. They don't ramble or preach, they spare us their quintuple subplots and swollen midsections.

For McEwan, "The Dead" is not simply a novella; it is "the perfect novella." "Joyce's genius apart, it was the particular demands of the novella, the way it lays on the writer a duty of unity and the pursuit of perfection, that brought him to shape in this fashion one of the loveliest fictions in the English language."

As a set of linked but independent stories, *Dubliners* shows the influence of two other early twentieth-century short-story collections: *The Untilled Field* (1903), by Irish writer George Moore, and Joseph Conrad's *Youth: A Narrative, and Two other Stories* (1902). The former, a short story collection in which specific themes and images recur throughout, contains two Dublin stories. The latter, in which *Heart of Darkness* was first published in its entirety, contains, sequentially, a tale of youth (the title narrative), one of maturity ("Heart of Darkness"), and one of old age ("The End of the Tether"), foreshadowing Joyce's organizational structure. Nonetheless, *Heart of Darkness* is so routinely read as a work of stand-alone fiction that its title is more often italicized than put in quotation marks. Though longer than "The Dead," it has no more claim to the status of novella than Joyce's story. Each functions independently, but ultimately forms one part of a larger whole.

While highlighting "The Dead" for those readers who wish to focus on this story (or for those courses in which it is not possible to cover all of *Dubliners*), the present volume also aims also to convey the story's significance as part of the larger work. Toward that end, we have included stories from each section (childhood, adolescence, maturity, and public life, as indicated above), as well as a range of contextual materials to help situate both the individual stories and the collection as a whole. We hope thus to provide readers with a strong sense of the literary and historical context out of which "The Dead" emerged, inviting the story's appreciation not only as "the perfect novella," but also as the capstone to one of the most important short-story collections ever written.

In 1904, Joyce also commenced *Stephen Hero*. Though this semi-autobiographical novel (or, rather, the surviving portion of the manuscript) was not published until after Joyce's death, it formed the basis of *A Portrait of the Artist as a Young Man*, which he began in 1907, the same year he abandoned its precursor. *Portrait* was first published serially in *The Egoist* from 1914 to 1915. The complete volume was published in 1916 by New York publisher B.W. Huebsch. Despite the support of major literary figures such as Yeats, H.G. Wells, and Ezra Pound, it had been rejected by every London publisher to whom Joyce had sent it—including Grant Richards.

The hero of *Portrait*, Stephen Dedalus, bears a striking similarity to Joyce himself. The novel details the artistic growth of a writer from childhood to the age of twenty, and outlines Joyce's artistic mission in life: to "record ... with extreme care" epiphanic moments of sublime self-awareness. It also extends Joyce's experiments with style, as the voice of the implied narrator changes and develops in correspondence with the development of the central character.

Ulysses details a day in Dublin life. Events in the novel follow the comings and goings of Stephen Dedalus, continuing the artistic journey on which Joyce set him in *A Portrait of the Artist as a Young Man*, and Leopold Bloom, the Jewish-Irish Everyman who is the hero of the novel. *Ulysses* takes as its model Homer's *Odyssey*; an everyday journey through the neighborhoods of Dublin becomes highly symbolic as Leopold Bloom follows a path that parallels that of Homer's hero Odysseus. Stephen Dedalus plays the role of Homer's Telemachus; Joyce imagines him an artist and visionary cut off from society. Joyce believed that Odysseus was perhaps the most well-rounded character in Western literature, embodying the best and the worst in human behavior, including courage, cowardice, intelligence, and deceit. Joyce's endeavors to portray these traits in his hero make Leopold Bloom one of the most warmly compelling characters in all of twentieth-century literature.

In form, each chapter is an ironic rewriting of a chapter from Homer's *Odyssey*, and is written in a broadly different literary style than the one that precedes it. The novel adopts a stream-of-consciousness approach that makes little or no distinction between what is happening externally and what takes place in a character's mind. Perspectives move fluidly from internal to external dialogue, from character to character, and from event to event, with little to indicate the change. The novel's central themes are those that recur in Joyce's work: the inner life of Dublin in all its beauty and hollowness, and the outsider status of characters (Leopold Bloom because of his Jewish background and Stephen Dedalus because of his artistic mission). This shared experience of Leopold and Stephen, and Stephen's figurative search for an absent father, link the two thematically throughout the story.

Portions of *Ulysses* were published serially in the *Little Review* beginning in 1918, but in 1920 publication ceased in the face of obscenity charges. (Initially, the U.S. Customs court objected to a masturbation scene; the court case centered on the book's use of profane language and its explicit portrayal of its characters' sexual thoughts and actions.) Not until 1922 was *Ulysses* published in complete form, and even then it was printed in Paris, but not in Britain or Ireland. An American edition was published in 1934, after a landmark court case decided the book was not pornography. The weary judge at the time acquiesced to the view that the book was a work of art, even if many readers would not understand it. A British edition of *Ulysses*, available to those in Northern Ireland but not in southern Ireland, finally appeared in 1937.

It was not until about 1920 that the Joyce family began to attain a modest level of financial security, largely the result of the support and patronage of several people who had as much faith in Joyce's genius as he himself did. The family moved from Trieste to Zurich in 1914, then to Paris in 1920, then back to Zurich in 1940. There, Joyce died of a perforated ulcer, just after seeing the publication of his final—and perhaps least understood—novel, *Finnegans Wake* (1939). In stylistic terms, the novel goes beyond the playful, self-conscious mode of *Ulysses* and enters a far more obscure territory. The title refers to a common folk song in which a laborer, Finnegan, falls and hits his head. His friends assume he is dead and hold a wake for him; he finally awakens after having whiskey spilled on him. *Finnegans Wake* is ostensibly the dream of Finnegan's successor, a Dublin Everyman with the initials H.C.E. (which stand for a variety of names, including Humphrey Chimpden Earwicker and Here Comes Everybody), and also features H.C.E.'s wife, A.L.P. (Anna Livia Plurabelle, Amnis Limina Permanent) and their twin sons, Shem and Shaun. Everything that occurs, and all the characters present, belong at least partially to the realm of dream. The novel's form relies on the cyclical view of history set out by Italian philosopher Giambattista Vico (1668–1744). The narrative is largely composed of multi-leveled puns that are fraught with symbolic meaning. Joyce used elements of English and no less than seven other languages to create the texture of the novel, reinventing not just the form of the novel but the structure of language itself in order to escape the stifling traditions in which he felt conventional language was steeped.

Joyce promised that his writing would "keep the professors busy," and in this he has succeeded, and continues to succeed, to an extent that even he might not have expected. For many years scholars were occupied with historical, cultural, and anthropological research into the background of Joyce's Dublin. While this research continues, developments in critical theory (such as psychoanalytic theory and postcolonial theory) have also opened up many new ways to interpret Joyce's texts. During his lifetime much of his work was, as one of Joyce's friends said, "outside of literature"; "literature" has since shifted to accommodate Joyce.

The Sisters

There was no hope for him this time: it was the third stroke. Night after night I had passed the house (it was vacation time) and studied the lighted square of window: and night after night I had found it lighted in the same way, faintly and evenly. If he was dead, I thought, I would see the reflection of candles on the darkened blind for I knew that two candles must be set at the head of a corpse. He had often said to me: *I am not long for this world*, and I had thought his words idle. Now I knew they were true. Every night as I gazed up at the window I said softly to myself the word *paralysis*. It had always sounded strangely in my ears like the word *gnomon* in the Euclid and the word *simony* in the catechism.[1] But now it sounded to me like the name of some maleficent and sinful being. It filled me with fear and yet I longed to be nearer to it and to look upon its deadly work.

Old Cotter was sitting at the fire, smoking, when I came downstairs to supper. While my aunt was ladling out my stirabout[2] he said as if returning to some former remark of his:

—No, I wouldn't say he was exactly ...... but there was something queer ..... there was something uncanny about him. I'll tell you my opinion....

He began to puff at his pipe, no doubt arranging his opinion in his mind. Tiresome old fool! When we knew him first he used to be rather interesting, talking of faints and worms;[3] but I soon grew tired of him and his endless stories about the distillery.

---

1   *gnomon*   Figure produced when a smaller parallelogram is removed from the corner of a larger parallelogram of the same shape;   *Euclid*   Greek geometrician (fl. 300 BCE), here referring to Euclid's *Elements*, a thirteen-book geometric treatise; see the illustration that follows this story;   *simony*   Exchange of something material for something spiritual, especially the purchase or sale of church positions or pardons for sins. The name derives from Simon Magus, a sorcerer who attempts to buy the power of transmission of the Holy Spirit in Acts 8.18–24;   *catechism*   Instruction in Christian doctrine, often in question and answer form.

2   *stirabout*   Porridge.

3   *faints and worms*   Terminology relating to the distillation of alcoholic beverages. Faints are the impure spirits produced early and late in the process. Worms are coiled condensation tubes.

—I have my own theory about it, he said. I think it was one of those ... peculiar cases.... But it's hard to say....

He began to puff again at his pipe without giving us his theory. My uncle saw me staring and said to me:

—Well, so your old friend is gone, you'll be sorry to hear.

—Who? said I.

—Father Flynn.

—Is he dead?

—Mr. Cotter here has just told us. He was passing by the house.

I knew that I was under observation so I continued eating as if the news had not interested me. My uncle explained to old Cotter:

—The youngster and he were great friends. The old chap taught him a great deal, mind you; and they say he had a great wish for him.[1]

—God have mercy on his soul, said my aunt piously.

Old Cotter looked at me for a while. I felt that his little beady black eyes were examining me but I would not satisfy him by looking up from my plate. He returned to his pipe and finally spat rudely into the grate.

—I wouldn't like children of mine, he said, to have too much to say to a man like that.

—How do you mean, Mr. Cotter? asked my aunt.

—What I mean is, said old Cotter, it's bad for children. My idea is: let a young lad run about and play with young lads of his own age and not be.... Am I right, Jack?

—That's my principle too, said my uncle. Let him learn to box his corner. That's what I'm always saying to that rosicrucian[2] there: take exercise. Why, when I was a nipper every morning of my life I had a cold bath, winter and summer. And that's what stands to me now. Education is all very fine and large..... Mr. Cotter might take a pick of that leg of mutton, he added to my aunt.

—No, no, not for me, said old Cotter.

My aunt brought the dish from the safe[3] and laid it on the table.

—But why do you think it's not good for children, Mr. Cotter? she asked.

---

1 *great wish for him* English version of an Irish phrase meaning "held him in great esteem."

2 *rosicrucian* I.e., dreamer; more specifically, a member of a secret society of religious mystics that has existed since at least the seventeenth century.

3 *safe* Food storage cabinet, typically kept in a cool part of the house.

—It's bad for children, said old Cotter, because their minds are so impressionable. When children see things like that, you know, it has an effect......

I crammed my mouth with stirabout for fear I might give utterance to my anger. Tiresome old rednosed imbecile!

It was late when I fell asleep. Though I was angry with old Cotter for alluding to me as a child I puzzled my head to extract meaning from his unfinished sentences. In the dark of my room I imagined that I saw again the heavy grey face of the paralytic. I drew the blankets over my head and tried to think of Christmas. But the grey face still followed me. It murmured and I understood that it desired to confess something. I felt my soul receding into some pleasant and vicious region and there again I found it waiting for me. It began to confess to me in a murmuring voice and I wondered why it smiled continually and why the lips were so moist with spittle. But then I remembered that it had died of paralysis and I felt that I too was smiling feebly as if to absolve the simoniac of his sin.[1]

The next morning after breakfast I went down to look at the little house in Great Britain Street.[2] It was an unassuming shop, registered under the vague name of *Drapery*. The drapery consisted mainly of children's bootees and umbrellas and on ordinary days a notice used to hang in the window, saying *Umbrellas Recovered*. No notice was visible now for the shutters were up. A crape bouquet was tied to the doorknocker with ribbon. Two poor women and a telegram boy were reading the card pinned on the crape. I also approached and read:

July 1st 1895
The Rev. James Flynn (formerly of S. Catherine's
Church, Meath Street)[3] aged sixty-five years.
R. I. P.

---

1   *absolve the ... his sin*   In Roman Catholicism, simony merited excommunication, and its absolution (forgiveness) would thus have to come from someone occupying a higher office than that of priest.
2   *Great Britain Street*   Now Parnell Street. Located in north-central Dublin, it was in a poor part of town in 1895.
3   *S. Catherine's ... Meath Street*   Catholic church in central Dublin.

The reading of the card persuaded me that he was dead and I was disturbed to find myself at check. Had he not been dead I would have gone into the little dark room behind the shop to find him sitting in his armchair by the fire, nearly smothered in his greatcoat. Perhaps my aunt would have given me a packet of high toast[1] for him and this present would have roused him from his stupefied doze. It was always I who emptied the packet into his black snuffbox for his hands trembled too much to allow him to do this without spilling half the snuff about the floor. Even as he raised his large trembling hand to his nose little clouds of smoke dribbled through his fingers over the front of his coat. It may have been these constant showers of snuff which gave his ancient priestly garments their green faded look for the red handkerchief, blackened as it always was with the snuffstains of a week, with which he tried to brush away the fallen grains was quite inefficacious.

I wished to go in and look at him but I had not the courage to knock. I walked away slowly along the sunny side of the street, reading all the theatrical advertisements in the shopwindows as I went. I found it strange that neither I nor the day seemed in a mourning mood and I felt even annoyed at discovering in myself a sensation of freedom as if I had been freed from something by his death. I wondered at this for, as my uncle had said the night before, he had taught me a great deal. He had studied in the Irish college in Rome[2] and he had taught me to pronounce Latin properly. He had told me stories about the catacombs and about Napoleon Bonaparte[3] and he had explained to me the meaning of the different ceremonies of the mass and of the different vestments worn by the priest. Sometimes he had amused himself by putting difficult questions to me, asking me what one should do in certain circumstances or whether such and such sins were mortal or venial[4] or only imperfections. His questions showed

---

1   *high toast*   Type of snuff.

2   *Irish college in Rome*   Irish seminary attended by only the most promising students.

3   *catacombs*   Underground passages in Rome, used by early Christians as burial sites;   *Napoleon Bonaparte*   French politician and military strategist (1769–1821) who made himself Emperor of France. During the Napoleonic Wars (1796–1815), the French Empire conquered and then lost much of Europe under his leadership.

4   *mortal or venial*   According to Catholic doctrine, a mortal sin is grave, made with full knowledge and consent, and punishable by eternal damnation. Venial sin is less grave, and/or made without knowledge and/or consent, and does not condemn one to damnation.

me how complex and mysterious were certain institutions of the church which I had always regarded as the simplest acts. The duties of the priest towards the eucharist and towards the secrecy of the confessional[1] seemed so grave to me that I wondered how anybody had ever found in himself the courage to undertake them: and I was not surprised when he told me that the fathers of the church[2] had written books as thick as the post office directory and as closely printed as the law notices in the newspaper elucidating all these intricate questions. Often when I thought of this I could make no answer or only a very foolish and halting one upon which he used to smile and nod his head twice or thrice. Sometimes he used to put me through the responses of the mass[3] which he had made me learn by heart: and as I pattered he used to smile pensively and nod his head, now and then pushing huge pinches of snuff up each nostril alternately. When he smiled he used to uncover his big discoloured teeth and let his tongue lie upon his lower lip—a habit which had made me feel uneasy in the beginning of our acquaintance before I knew him well.

As I walked along in the sun I remembered old Cotter's words and tried to remember what had happened afterwards in the dream. I remembered that I had noticed long velvet curtains and a swinging lamp of antique fashion. I felt that I had been very far away, in some land where the customs were strange, in Persia,[4] I thought....... But I could not remember the end of the dream.

In the evening my aunt took me with her to visit the house of mourning. It was after sunset but the window panes of the houses that looked to the west reflected the tawny gold of a great bank of clouds. Nannie received us in the hall and, as it would have been unseemly to have shouted at her, my aunt shook hands with her for all. The old woman pointed upwards interrogatively and, on my aunt's nodding, proceeded to toil up the narrow staircase before us, her bowed head being scarcely above the level of the banister rail. At

---

1 *eucharist* Holy Communion or Mass; that is, the consumption of consecrated bread and wine in memory of Christ's sacrifice. In Roman Catholicism, the bread and wine are believed to be transformed into the blood and body of Christ; *confessional* Place where a priest hears confession, which he is sworn to keep secret.
2 *fathers of the church* Early Christian theologians.
3 *responses of the mass* Formal responses made to a priest during Mass.
4 *Persia* Now Iran.

the first landing she stopped and beckoned us forward encouragingly towards the open door of the deadroom. My aunt went in and the old woman, seeing that I hesitated to enter, began to beckon to me again repeatedly with her hand.

I went in on tiptoe. The room through the lace end of the blind was suffused with dusky golden light amid which the candles looked like pale thin flames. He had been coffined. Nannie gave the lead and we three knelt down at the foot of the bed. I pretended to pray but I could not gather my thoughts because the old woman's mutterings distracted me. I noticed how clumsily her skirt was hooked at the back and how the heels of her cloth boots were trodden down all to one side. The fancy came to me that the old priest was smiling as he lay there in his coffin.

But no. When we rose and went up to the head of the bed I saw that he was not smiling. There he lay, solemn and copious, vested as for the altar, his large hands loosely retaining a chalice.[1] His face was very truculent, grey and massive, with black cavernous nostrils and circled by a scanty white fur. There was a heavy odour in the room, the flowers.

We blessed ourselves and came away. In the little room downstairs we found Eliza seated in his armchair in state. I groped my way towards my usual chair in the corner while Nannie went to the sideboard and brought out a decanter of sherry and some wineglasses. She set these on the table and invited us to take a little glass of wine. Then, at her sister's bidding, she poured out the sherry into the glasses and passed them to us. She pressed me to take some cream crackers also but I declined because I thought I would make too much noise eating them. She seemed to be somewhat disappointed at my refusal and went over quietly to the sofa where she sat down behind her sister. No-one spoke: we all gazed at the empty fireplace.

My aunt waited until Eliza sighed and then said:

—Ah, well, he's gone to a better world.

Eliza sighed again and bowed her head in assent. My aunt fingered the stem of her wineglass before sipping a little.

—Did he ..... peacefully? she asked.

---

1   *chalice*   Vessel for consecrated wine used during the Eucharist.

—O, quite peacefully, ma'am, said Eliza. You couldn't tell when the breath went out of him. He had a beautiful death, God be praised.

—And everything ....?[1]

—Father O'Rourke was in with him a-Tuesday and anointed him and prepared him and all.

—He knew then?

—He was quite resigned.

—He looks quite resigned, said my aunt.

—That's what the woman we had in to wash him said. She said he just looked as if he was asleep, he looked that peaceful and resigned. No-one would think he'd make such a beautiful corpse.

—Yes, indeed, said my aunt.

She sipped a little more from her glass and said:

—Well, Miss Flynn, at any rate it must be a great comfort for you to know that you did all you could for him. You were both very kind to him, I must say.

Eliza smoothed her dress over her knees.

—Ah, poor James! she said. God knows we done all we could as poor as we are. We wouldn't see him want anything while he was in it.

Nannie had leaned her head against the sofa pillow and seemed about to fall asleep.

—There's poor Nannie, said Eliza, looking at her, she's wore out. All the work we had, she and me, getting in the woman to wash him and then laying him out and then the coffin and then arranging about the mass in the chapel! Only for Father O'Rourke I don't know what we'd have done at all. It was him brought us all them flowers and them two candlesticks out of the chapel and wrote out the notice for the *Freeman's General*[2] and took charge of all the papers for the cemetery and poor James's insurance.

—Wasn't that good of him? said my aunt

Eliza closed her eyes and shook her head slowly.

—Ah, there's no friends like the old friends, she said, when all is said and done, no friends that a body can trust.

---

1 *And everything ....?* The speaker is asking whether the priest received his Last Rites, preparing his body and soul for death.

2 *Freeman's General* Misnomer for *The Freeman's Journal and National Press.*

—Indeed, that's true, said my aunt. And I'm sure now that he's gone to his eternal reward he won't forget you and all your kindness to him.

—Ah, poor James! said Eliza. He was no great trouble to us. You wouldn't hear him in the house any more than now. Still, I know he's gone and all that.....

—It's when it's all over that you'll miss him, said my aunt.

—I know that, said Eliza. I won't be bringing him in his cup of beeftea[1] any more nor you, ma'am, sending him his snuff. Ah, poor James!

She stopped, as if she were communing with the past, and then said shrewdly:

—Mind you, I noticed there was something queer coming over him latterly. Whenever I'd bring in his soup to him there I'd find him with his breviary[2] fallen on the floor, lying back in the chair and his mouth open.

She laid a finger against her nose and frowned: then she continued:

—But still and all he kept on saying that before the summer was over he'd go out for a drive one fine day just to see the old house again where we were all born down in Irishtown[3] and take me and Nannie with him. If we could only get one of them newfangled carriages that makes no noise that Father O'Rourke told him about—them with the rheumatic wheels[4]—for the day cheap, he said, at Johnny Rush's over the way there and drive out the three of us together of a Sunday evening. He had his mind set on that.... Poor James!

—The Lord have mercy on his soul! said my aunt.

Eliza took out her handkerchief and wiped her eyes with it. Then she put it back again in her pocket and gazed into the empty grate for some time without speaking.

—He was too scrupulous always, she said. The duties of the priesthood was too much for him. And then his life was, you might say, crossed.

---

1 *beeftea*   Beef broth, a drink frequently given to sick people.

2 *breviary*   Book of daily prayers.

3 *Irishtown*   South Dublin, where many poor people then lived.

4 *rheumatic wheels*   The speaker means "pneumatic tires": rubber tires filled with compressed air.

—Yes, said my aunt, he was a disappointed man. You could see that.

A silence took possession of the little room and under cover of it I approached the table and tasted my sherry and then returned quietly to my chair in the corner. Eliza seemed to have fallen into a deep revery. We waited respectfully for her to break the silence: and after a long pause she said slowly:

—It was that chalice he broke.... That was what was the beginning of it. Of course, they say it was all right, that it contained nothing,[1] I mean. But still .... They say it was the boy's[2] fault. But poor James was so nervous, God be merciful to him!

—And was that it? said my aunt. I heard something........

Eliza nodded.

—That affected his mind, she said. After that he began to mope by himself, talking to no-one and wandering about by himself. So one night he was wanted for to go on a call and they couldn't find him anywhere. They looked high up and low down and still they couldn't see a sight of him anywhere. So then the clerk suggested to try the chapel. So then they got the keys and opened the chapel and the clerk and Father O'Rourke and another priest that was there brought in a light for to look for him..... And what do you think but there he was, sitting up by himself in the dark in his confession box, wideawake and laughing-like softly to himself?

She stopped suddenly as if to listen. I too listened but there was no sound in the house and I knew that the old priest was lying still in his coffin as we had seen him, solemn and truculent in death, an idle chalice on his breast.

Eliza resumed:

—Wideawake and laughing-like to himself.... So then of course when they saw that that made them think that there was something gone wrong with him.....

---

1 *contained nothing* The concern is that it might have contained consecrated wine.
2 *the boy* I.e., the altar boy, whose tasks sometimes include carrying and cleaning the chalice.

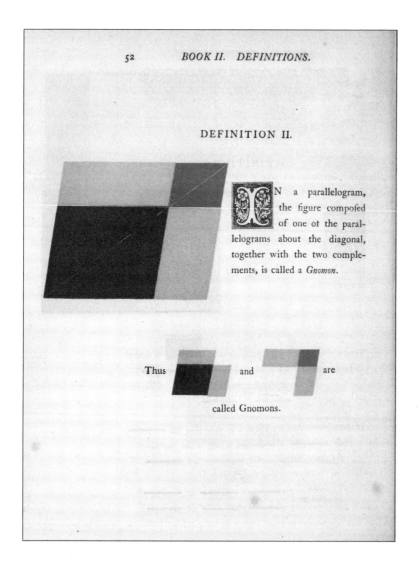

Definition of "*gnomon*" from Oliver Byrne's 1847 edition of *The First Six Books of the Elements of Euclid*. This popular edition, published by Pickering, is likely the one that Joyce—and the unnamed narrator of "The Sisters"—would have known.

Araby[1]

North Richmond Street, being blind,[2] was a quiet street except at the hour when the Christian Brothers' School set the boys free. An uninhabited house of two storeys stood at the blind end, detached from its neighbours in a square ground. The other houses of the street, conscious of decent lives within them, gazed at one another with brown imperturbable faces.

The former tenant of our house, a priest, had died in the back drawingroom. Air, musty from having been long enclosed, hung in all the rooms and the waste room behind the kitchen was littered with old useless papers. Among these I found a few papercovered books, the pages of which were curled and damp: *The Abbot* by Walter Scott, *The Devout Communicant* and *The Memoirs of Vidocq*.[3] I liked the last best because its leaves were yellow. The wild garden behind the house contained a central apple tree and a few straggling bushes under one of which I found the late tenant's rusty bicycle pump. He had been a very charitable priest; in his will he had left all his money to institutions and the furniture of his house to his sister.

When the short days of winter came dusk fell before we had well eaten our dinners. When we met in the street the houses had grown sombre. The space of sky above us was the colour of everchanging violet and towards it the lamps of the street lifted their feeble lanterns. The cold air stung us and we played till our bodies glowed. Our shouts echoed in the silent street. The career of our play brought us through the dark muddy lanes behind the houses where we ran the gantlet of the rough tribes from the cottages, to the back doors of the dark dripping gardens where odours arose from the ashpits, to the dark odorous stables where a coachman smoothed and combed the horse or shook music from the buckled harness. When we returned

---

1 *Araby* Billed as a "Grand Oriental Fête," "Araby in Dublin" was an 1894 charity bazaar. See also appendix E.2 in the "In Context" materials at the end of this volume.
2 *being blind* Being a dead end.
3 *The Abbot* 1820 historical novel by Scottish novelist Walter Scott; *The Devout Communicant* Probably referring to a Catholic religious manual written by Pacificus Baker (1695–1774), an English Franciscan; *The Memoirs of Vidocq* 1828 text possibly written by the titular subject, François-Eugène Vidocq, a French criminal turned detective.

to the street light from the kitchen windows had filled the areas.[1] If my uncle was seen turning the corner we hid in the shadow until we had seen him safely housed. Or if Mangan's sister[2] came out on the doorstep to call her brother in to his tea we watched her from our shadow peer up and down the street. We waited to see whether she would remain or go in and if she remained we left our shadow and walked up to Mangan's steps resignedly. She was waiting for us, her figure defined by the light from the half-opened door. Her brother always teased her before he obeyed and I stood by the railings looking at her. Her dress swung as she moved her body and the soft rope of her hair tossed from side to side.

Every morning I lay on the floor in the front parlour watching her door. The blind was pulled down to within an inch of the sash so that I could not be seen. When she came out on the doorstep my heart leaped. I ran to the hall, seized my books and followed her. I kept her brown figure always in my eye and when we came near the point at which our ways diverged I quickened my pace and passed her. This happened morning after morning. I had never spoken to her except for a few casual words and yet her name was like a summons to all my foolish blood.

Her image accompanied me even in places the most hostile to romance. On Saturday evenings when my aunt went marketing I had to go to carry some of the parcels. We walked through the flaring streets, jostled by drunken men and bargaining women, amid the curses of labourers, the shrill litanies of shop boys who stood on guard by the barrels of pigs' cheeks, the nasal chanting of street singers who sang a *come-all-you* about O'Donovan Rossa or a ballad about the troubles in our native land.[3] These noises converged in a single sensation of life for me: I imagined that I bore my chalice safely through a throng of foes. Her name sprang to my lips at moments in strange prayers and praises which I myself did not

---

1   *areas*   Spaces between the railings and the fronts of houses, below street level.

2   *Mangan's sister*   Likely an allusion to Irish Romantic poet James Clarence Mangan (1803–49), about whom Joyce presented a paper in 1902. See also appendices A.1 and D.1 in the "In Context" materials at the end of this volume.

3   *come-all-you*   Song or ballad, many of which begin with this refrain;   *O'Donovan Rossa*   Jeremiah O'Donovan Rossa (1831–1915) was an Irish nationalist imprisoned for revolutionary activities, later granted amnesty and exiled to America;   *the troubles in our native land*   For the most part this refers to the issue of Irish independence from England, a question over which the Irish were themselves divided.

understand. My eyes were often full of tears (I could not tell why) and at times a flood from my heart seemed to pour itself out into my bosom. I thought little of the future. I did not know whether I would ever speak to her or not or, if I spoke to her, how I could tell her of my confused adoration. But my body was like a harp and her words and gestures were like fingers running upon the wires.

One evening I went into the back drawingroom in which the priest had died. It was a dark rainy evening and there was no sound in the house. Through one of the broken panes I heard the rain impinge upon the earth, the fine incessant needles of water playing in the sodden beds. Some distant lamp or lighted window gleamed below me. I was thankful that I could see so little. All my senses seemed to desire to veil themselves and, feeling that I was about to slip from them, I pressed the palms of my hands together until they trembled, murmuring: *O love! O love!* many times.

At last she spoke to me. When she addressed the first words to me I was so confused that I did not know what to answer. She asked me was I going to *Araby*. I forget whether I answered yes or no. It would be a splendid bazaar, she said; she would love to go.

—And why can't you? I asked.

While she spoke she turned a silver bracelet round and round her wrist. She could not go, she said, because there would be a retreat that week in her convent.[1] Her brother and two other boys were fighting for their caps and I was alone at the railings. She held one of the spikes, bowing her head towards me. The light from the lamp opposite our door caught the white curve of her neck, lit up the hair that rested there and, falling, lit up the hand upon the railing. It fell over one side of her dress and caught the white border of a petticoat, just visible as she stood at ease.

—It's well for you, she said.

—If I go, I said, I will bring you something.

What innumerable follies laid waste my waking and sleeping thoughts after that evening! I wished to annihilate the tedious intervening days. I chafed against the work of school. At night in my bedroom and by day in the classroom her image came between me and the page I strove to read. The syllables of the word *Araby* were called to me through the silence in which my soul luxuriated and

---

1 *convent* I.e., convent school.

cast an eastern enchantment over me. I asked for leave to go to the bazaar on Saturday night. My aunt was surprised and hoped it was not some freemason affair.[1] I answered few questions in class. I watched my master's face pass from amiability to sternness; he hoped I was not beginning to idle. I could not call my wandering thoughts together. I had hardly any patience with the serious work of life which, now that it stood between me and my desire, seemed to me child's play, ugly monotonous child's play.

On Saturday morning I reminded my uncle that I wished to go to the bazaar in the evening. He was fussing at the hallstand, looking for the hatbrush, and answered me curtly:

—Yes, boy, I know.

As he was in the hall I could not go into the front parlour and lie at the window. I left the house in bad humour and walked slowly towards the school. The air was pitilessly raw and already my heart misgave me.

When I came home to dinner my uncle had not yet been home. Still it was early. I sat staring at the clock for some time and when its ticking began to irritate me I left the room. I mounted the staircase and gained the upper part of the house. The high cold empty gloomy rooms liberated me and I went from room to room singing. From the front window I saw my companions playing below in the street. Their cries reached me weakened and indistinct and, leaning my forehead against the cool glass, I looked over at the dark house where she lived. I may have stood there for an hour seeing nothing but the brownclad figure cast by my imagination, touched discreetly by the lamplight at the curved neck, at the hand upon the railings and at the border below the dress.

When I came downstairs again I found Mrs. Mercer sitting at the fire. She was an old garrulous woman, a pawnbroker's widow who collected used stamps for some pious purpose. I had to endure the gossip of the teatable. The meal was prolonged beyond an hour and still my uncle did not come. Mrs. Mercer stood up to go: she was sorry she couldn't wait any longer but it was after eight o'clock and she did not like to be out late as the night air was bad for her. When

---

1 *freemason affair* Affiliated with the Freemasons, a secret society originally made up of skilled stone-workers. The society was said to be anti-Catholic, and the Archbishop of Dublin had decreed that any Catholics caught at a freemason bazaar could be excommunicated.

she had gone I began to walk up and down the room, clenching my fists. My aunt said:

—I'm afraid you may put off your bazaar for this night of Our Lord.

At nine o'clock I heard my uncle's latchkey in the halldoor. I heard him talking to himself and heard the hallstand rocking when it had received the weight of his overcoat. I could interpret these signs. When he was midway through his dinner I asked him to give me the money to go to the bazaar. He had forgotten.

—The people are in bed and after their first sleep now, he said.

I did not smile. My aunt said to him energetically:

—Can't you give him the money and let him go? You've kept him late enough as it is.

My uncle said he was very sorry he had forgotten. He said he believed in the old saying: *All work and no play makes Jack a dull boy.* He asked me where I was going and when I had told him a second time he asked me did I know *The Arab's Farewell to his Steed.*[1] When I left the kitchen he was about to recite the opening lines of the piece to my aunt.

I held a florin tightly in my hand as I strode down Buckingham Street towards the station. The sight of the streets thronged with buyers and glaring with gas recalled to me the purpose of my journey. I took my seat in a third class carriage of a deserted train. After an intolerable delay the train moved out of the station slowly. It crept onward among ruinous houses and over the twinkling river. At Westland Row Station a crowd of people pressed at the carriage doors; but the porters moved them back, saying that it was a special train for the bazaar. I remained alone in the bare carriage. In a few minutes the train drew up beside an improvised wooden platform. I passed out on to the road and saw by the lighted dial of a clock that it was ten minutes to ten. In front of me was a large building which displayed the magical name.

I could not find any sixpenny entrance[2] and, fearing that the bazaar would be closed, I passed in quickly through a turnstile, handing a shilling to a wearylooking man. I found myself in a big hall girdled at half its height by a gallery. Nearly all the stalls were

---

1   *The Arab's ... his Steed*   Popular romantic poem by Caroline Norton (1808–77).

2   *sixpenny entrance*   Discounted entrance for the young.

closed and the greater part of the hall was in darkness. I recognised a silence like that which pervades a church after a service. I walked into the centre of the bazaar timidly. A few people were gathered about the stalls which were still open. Before a curtain over which the words *Café Chantant*[1] were written in coloured lamps two men were counting money on a salver. I listened to the fall of the coins.

Remembering with difficulty why I had come I went over to one of the stalls and examined porcelain vases and flowered teasets. At the door of the stall a young lady was talking and laughing with two young gentlemen. I remarked their English accents and listened vaguely to their conversation.

—O, I never said such a thing!

—O, but you did!

—O, but I didn't!

—Didn't she say that?

—She did. I heard her.

—O, there's a … fib!

Observing me the young lady came over and asked me did I wish to buy anything. The tone of her voice was not encouraging: she seemed to have spoken to me out of a sense of duty. I looked humbly at the great jars that stood like eastern guards at either side of the dark entrance to her stall and murmured:

—No, thank you.

The young lady changed the position of one of the vases and went back to the two young men. They began to talk of the same subject. Once or twice the young lady glanced at me over her shoulder.

I lingered before her stall, though I knew my stay was useless, to make my interest in her wares seem the more real. Then I turned away slowly and walked down the middle of the bazaar. I allowed the two pennies to fall against the sixpence in my pocket. I heard a voice call from one end of the gallery that the light was out. The upper part of the hall was now completely dark.

Gazing up into the darkness I saw myself as a creature driven and derided by vanity: and my eyes burned with anguish and anger.

---

1   *Café Chantant*   Café that provides musical entertainment.

Magnificent Representation

OF

AN ORIENTAL CITY.

CAIRO DONKEYS & DONKEY BOYS,

AN ARAB ENCAMPMENT.

INTERNATIONAL TUG-OF-WAR

DANCES BY 250 TRAINED CHILDREN.

Eastern Magic from the Egyptian Hall, London.

CAFE CHANTANT, WITH ALL THE LATEST PARISIAN SUCCESSES.

SKIRT DANCING up to Date.

TABLEAUX. THEATRICALS. CHRISTY MINSTRELS.

GRAND THEATRE OF VARIETIES,

"THE ALHAMBRA," An Orchestra of 50 Performers.

Switchback Railways and Roundabouts.

" *MENOTTI,*" *The King of the Air,*

THE GREAT STOCKHOLM WONDER.

BICYCLE POLO. RIFLE & CLAY PIGEON SHOOTING.

DANCING.

THE EUTERPEAN LADIES' ORCHESTRA.

EIGHT MILITARY BANDS,

Magnificent Displays of Fireworks,

BY BROCK, OF THE CRYSTAL PALACE, LONDON.

ADMISSION • • ONE SHILLING.

Back of *Araby in Dublin Official Catalogue*, 1894. For a week in May 1894, Dubliners flocked to see "Araby in Dublin," which was billed as a "Grand Oriental Fête." Drawing on Orientalist tropes about the mystical East that had long circulated in Europe (see introduction, page 12), it included displays such as "an Oriental City" and "an Arab encampment" and events such as "eastern magic" and "skirt dancing." The fête attracted nearly one-third of Dublin's residents, netted approximately £10,000 for charity, and likely served as the model for the bazaar in Joyce's "Araby."

Eveline

She sat at the window watching the evening invade the avenue. Her head was leaned against the window curtains and in her nostrils was the odour of dusty cretonne.[1] She was tired.

Few people passed. The man out of the last house passed on his way home; she heard his footsteps clacking along the concrete pavement and afterwards crunching on the cinder path before the new red houses. One time there used to be a field there in which they used to play every evening with other people's children. Then a man from Belfast bought the field and built houses in it—not like their little brown houses but bright brick houses with shining roofs. The children of the avenue used to play together in that field—the Devines, the Waters, the Dunns, little Keogh the cripple, she and her brothers and sisters. Ernest, however, never played: he was too grown up. Her father used often to hunt them in out of the field with his blackthorn stick but usually little Keogh used to keep nix[2] and call out when he saw her father coming. Still they seemed to have been rather happy then. Her father was not so bad then, and besides her mother was alive. That was a long time ago; she and her brothers and sisters were all grown up; her mother was dead. Tizzie Dunn was dead, too, and the Waters had gone back to England. Everything changes. Now she was going to go away like the others, to leave her home.

Home! She looked round the room reviewing all its familiar objects which she had dusted once a week for so many years, wondering where on earth all the dust came from. Perhaps she would never see again those familiar objects from which she had never dreamed of being divided. And yet during all those years she had never found out the name of the priest whose yellowing photograph hung on the wall above the broken harmonium[3] beside the coloured print of the promises made to Blessed Margaret Mary

---

1   *cretonne*   Thick, unglazed, cotton fabric often used for chair covers and curtains.
2   *keep nix*   Keep watch.
3   *harmonium*   Type of reed organ.

Alacoque.[1] He had been a school friend of her father's. Whenever he showed the photograph to a visitor her father used to pass it with a casual word:

—He is in Melbourne now.

She had consented to go away, to leave her home. Was that wise? She tried to weigh each side of the question. In her home anyway she had shelter and food; she had those whom she had known all her life about her. Of course she had to work hard both in the house and at business. What would they say of her in the stores when they found out that she had run away with a fellow? Say she was a fool, perhaps; and her place would be filled up by advertisement. Miss Gavan would be glad. She had always had an edge on her, especially whenever there were people listening.

—Miss Hill, don't you see these ladies are waiting?

—Look lively, Miss Hill, please.

She would not cry many tears at leaving the stores.

But in her new home, in a distant unknown country, it would not be like that. Then she would be married—she, Eveline. People would treat her with respect then. She would not be treated as her mother had been. Even now, though she was over nineteen, she sometimes felt herself in danger of her father's violence. She knew it was that that had given her the palpitations. When they were growing up he had never gone for her, like he used to go for Harry and Ernest, because she was a girl; but latterly he had begun to threaten her and say what he would do to her only for her dead mother's sake. And now she had nobody to protect her. Ernest was dead and Harry, who was in the church decorating business, was nearly always down somewhere in the country. Besides, the invariable squabble for money on Saturday nights had begun to weary her unspeakably. She always gave her entire wages—seven shillings—and Harry always sent up what he could but the trouble was to get any money from her father. He said she used to squander the money, that she had no head, that he wasn't going to give her his hard earned money to throw about the streets and much more for

---

1 *Blessed Margaret Mary Alacoque* French nun who lived from 1647–90, was beatified in 1864, and canonized in 1920. She subjected herself to extreme self-mortification and received visions from Jesus Christ, who she said promised blessings to those who practiced devotion to his Sacred Heart.

he was usually fairly bad of a Saturday night. In the end he would give her the money and ask her had she any intention of buying Sunday's dinner. Then she had to rush out as quickly as she could and do her marketing, holding her black leather purse tightly in her hand as she elbowed her way through the crowds and returning home late under her load of provisions. She had hard work to keep the house together and to see that the two young children who had been left to her charge went to school regularly and got their meals regularly. It was hard work—a hard life—but now that she was about to leave it she did not find it a wholly undesirable life.

She was about to explore another life with Frank. Frank was very kind, manly, openhearted. She was to go away with him by the night boat to be his wife and to live with him in Buenos Ayres[1] where he had a home waiting for her. How well she remembered the first time she had seen him; he was lodging in a house on the main road where she used to visit. It seemed a few weeks ago. He was standing at the gate, his peaked cap pushed back on his head and his hair tumbled forward over a face of bronze. Then they had come to know each other. He used to meet her outside the stores every evening and see her home. He took her to see the *Bohemian Girl*[2] and she felt elated as she sat in an unaccustomed part of the theatre with him. He was awfully fond of music and sang a little. People knew that they were courting and when he sang about the lass that loves a sailor[3] she always felt pleasantly confused. He used to call her Poppens out of fun. First of all it had been an excitement for her to have a fellow and then she had begun to like him. He had tales of distant countries. He had started as a deck boy at a pound a month on a ship of the Allan line[4] going out to Canada. He told her the names of the ships he had been on and the names of the different services. He had sailed through the Straits of Mag-

---

1 *Buenos Ayres* Argentina's capital, today spelled "Buenos Aires." "Going to Buenos Aires" was formerly a euphemism for becoming a prostitute, which may be significant to this story, given that *Eveline* was the title of an anonymous mid-Victorian erotic novel (exact date unknown).

2 *Bohemian Girl* 1843 opera by Dubliner Michael Balfe.

3 *the lass that loves a sailor* Title of a song by English writer Charles Dibdin (1745–1814).

4 *the Allan line* The Allan Steamship Company, founded in 1852 by Sir Hugh Allan, made weekly departures from Liverpool to the western coast of Canada (with stops along the way, including Buenos Aires).

ellan and he told her stories of the terrible Patagonians.[1] He had fallen on his feet in Buenos Ayres, he said, and had come over to the old country just for a holiday. Of course, her father had found out the affair and had forbidden her to have anything to say to him:

—I know these sailor chaps, he said.

One day he had quarrelled with Frank and after that she had to meet her lover secretly.

The evening deepened in the avenue. The white of two letters in her lap grew indistinct. One was to Harry, the other was to her father. Ernest had been her favourite but she liked Harry too. Her father was becoming old lately, she noticed; he would miss her. Sometimes he could be very nice. Not long before, when she had been laid up for a day, he had read her out a ghost story and made toast for her at the fire. Another day, when their mother was alive, they had all gone for a picnic to the Hill of Howth.[2] She remembered her father putting on her mother's bonnet to make the children laugh.

Her time was running out but she continued to sit by the window, leaning her head against the window curtain, inhaling the odour of dusty cretonne. Down far in the avenue she could hear a street organ playing. She knew the air. Strange that it should come that very night to remind her of the promise to her mother, her promise to keep the home together as long as she could. She remembered the last night of her mother's illness; she was again in the close dark room at the other side of the hall and outside she heard a melancholy air of Italy. The organ player had been ordered to go away and given sixpence. She remembered her father strutting back into the sickroom saying:

—Damned Italians! coming over here!

As she mused the pitiful vision of her mother's life laid its spell on the very quick of her being—that life of commonplace sacrifices closing in final craziness. She trembled as she heard again her mother's voice saying constantly with foolish insistence:

---

1 *the terrible Patagonians* Refers either to the strong, unpredictable Patagonian winds in the Strait of Magellan, or to the inhabitants of the tip of South America, whom the Europeans associated with barbarity.

2 *Hill of Howth* Located northeast of Dublin, on the Howth peninsula.

—Derevaun Seraun! Derevaun Seraun![1]

She stood up in a sudden impulse of terror. Escape! She must escape! Frank would save her. He would give her life, perhaps love too. But she wanted to live. Why should she be unhappy? She had a right to happiness. Frank would take her in his arms, fold her in his arms. He would save her.

*   *   *

She stood among the swaying crowd in the station at the North Wall.[2] He held her hand and she knew that he was speaking to her, saying something about the passage over and over again. The station was full of soldiers with brown baggages. Through the wide doors of the sheds she caught a glimpse of the black mass of the boat lying in beside the quay wall, with illumined portholes. She answered nothing. She felt her cheek pale and cold and out of a maze of distress she prayed to God to direct her, to show her what was her duty. The boat blew a long mournful whistle into the mist. If she went, tomorrow she would be on the sea with Frank, steaming towards Buenos Ayres. Their passage had been booked. Could she still draw back after all he had done for her? Her distress awoke a nausea in her body and she kept moving her lips in silent fervent prayer.

A bell clanged upon her heart. She felt him seize her hand:

—Come!

All the seas of the world tumbled about her heart. He was drawing her into them: he would drown her. She gripped with both hands at the iron railing.

—Come!

No! No! No! It was impossible. Her hands clutched the iron in frenzy. Amid the seas she sent a cry of anguish.

—Eveline! Evvy!

He rushed beyond the barrier and called to her to follow. He was shouted at to go on but he still called to her. She set her white face to him, passive, like a helpless animal. Her eyes gave him no sign of love or farewell or recognition.

---

1   *Derevaun Seraun*   The meaning of this phrase, if there is one, is uncertain. While some scholars believe it to be garbled Irish, others assert it is gibberish.
2   *North Wall*   Quay along Dublin Port.

Irish sailors at the turn of the century. Frank, who courts Eveline in Joyce's story of the same name, was probably a sailor.

A Little Cloud[1]

Eight years before he had seen his friend off at the North Wall[2] and wished him godspeed. Gallaher had got on. You could tell that at once by his travelled air, his well-cut tweed suit and fearless accent. Few fellows had talents like his and fewer still could remain unspoiled by such success. Gallaher's heart was in the right place and he had deserved to win. It was something to have a friend like that.

Little Chandler's thoughts ever since lunchtime had been of his meeting with Gallaher, of Gallaher's invitation and of the great city London where Gallaher lived. He was called Little Chandler because, though he was but slightly under the average stature, he gave one the idea of being a little man. His hands were white and small, his frame was fragile, his voice was quiet and his manners were refined. He took the greatest care of his fair silken hair and moustache and used perfume discreetly on his handkerchief. The half moons of his nails were perfect and when he smiled you caught a glimpse of a row of childish white teeth.

As he sat at his desk in the King's Inns[3] he thought what changes those eight years had brought. The friend whom he had known under a shabby and necessitous guise had become a brilliant figure on the London press. He turned often from his tiresome writing to gaze out of the office window. The glow of a late autumn sunset covered the grass plots and walks. It cast a shower of kindly golden dust on the untidy nurses and decrepit old men who drowsed on the benches; it flickered upon all the moving figures—on the children who ran screaming along the gravel paths and on everyone who passed through the gardens. He watched the scene and thought of life; and (as always happened when he thought of life) he became sad. A gentle melancholy took possession of him. He felt how useless it was to

---

1 *A Little Cloud* In I Kings 18.44, "a little cloud out of the sea" signals the end of a great famine.
2 *North Wall* Quay along Dublin port.
3 *the King's Inns* Institution of legal education and site of bureaucratic offices in central Dublin.

struggle against fortune, this being the burden of wisdom which the ages had bequeathed to him.

He remembered the books of poetry upon his shelves at home. He had bought them in his bachelor days and many an evening, as he sat in the little room off the hall, he had been tempted to take one down from the bookshelf and read out something to his wife. But shyness had always held him back, and so the books had remained on their shelves. At times he repeated lines to himself and this consoled him.

When his hour had struck he stood up and took leave of his desk and of his fellow clerks punctiliously. He emerged from under the feudal arch of the King's Inns, a neat modest figure, and walked swiftly down Henrietta Street.[1] The golden sunset was waning and the air had grown sharp. A horde of grimy children populated the street. They stood or ran in the roadway or crawled up the steps before the gaping doors or squatted like mice upon the thresholds. Little Chandler gave them no thought. He picked his way deftly through all that minute verminlike life and under the shadow of the gaunt spectral mansions in which the old nobility of Dublin had roistered.[2] No memory of the past touched him, for his mind was full of a present joy.

He had never been in Corless's[3] but he knew the value of the name. He knew that people went there after the theatre to eat oysters and drink liqueurs; and he had heard that the waiters there spoke French and German. Walking swiftly by at night he had seen cabs drawn up before the door and richly dressed ladies, escorted by cavaliers, alight and enter quickly. They wore noisy dresses and many wraps. Their faces were powdered and they caught up their dresses, when they touched earth, like alarmed Atalantas.[4] He had always passed without turning his head to look. It was his habit to walk swiftly in the

---

1 *Henrietta Street* Street with low-rent buildings, located near the King's Inns. All streets named in this story are located in Dublin.

2 *roistered* In this case, lived extravagantly and behaved boisterously.

3 *Corless's* Well-known hotel and restaurant in central Dublin.

4 *Atalantas* According to Greek mythology, Atalanta was a much sought-after princess who would only marry the man who could beat her in a footrace. Victorian artists depicted her holding her dress aloft as she ran.

street even by day and whenever he found himself in the city late at night he hurried on his way apprehensively and excitedly. Sometimes, however, he courted the causes of his fear. He chose the darkest and narrowest streets and, as he walked boldly forward, the silence that was spread about his footsteps troubled him, the wandering silent figures troubled him, and at times a sound of low fugitive laughter made him tremble like a leaf.

He turned to the right towards Capel Street. Ignatius Gallaher on the London press! Who would have thought it possible eight years before? Still, now that he reviewed the past, Little Chandler could remember many signs of future greatness in his friend. People used to say that Ignatius Gallaher was wild. Of course, he did mix with a rakish set of fellows at that time, drank freely and borrowed money on all sides. In the end he had got mixed up in some shady affair, some money transaction: at least, that was one version of his flight. But nobody denied him talent. There was always a certain … something in Ignatius Gallaher that impressed you in spite of yourself. Even when he was out at elbows and at his wits' end for money he kept up a bold face. Little Chandler remembered (and the remembrance brought a slight flush of pride to his cheek) one of Ignatius Gallaher's sayings when he was in a tight corner:

—Half time now, boys, he used to say lightheartedly. Where's my considering cap?

That was Ignatius Gallaher all out; and, damn it, you couldn't but admire him for it.

Little Chandler quickened his pace. For the first time in his life he felt himself superior to the people he passed. For the first time his soul revolted against the dull inelegance of Capel Street. There was no doubt about it: if you wanted to succeed you had to go away. You could do nothing in Dublin. As he crossed Grattan Bridge he looked down the river towards the lower quays and pitied the poor stunted houses. They seemed to him a band of tramps huddled together along the river banks, their old coats covered with dust and soot, stupefied by the panorama of sunset and waiting for the first chill of night to bid them arise, shake themselves and begone. He wondered whether he could write a poem to express his idea. Perhaps Gallaher might be able to get it into some London paper for him. Could he write something original? He was not sure what idea he wished to express but the thought that a poetic moment had touched him took life within him like an infant hope. He stepped onward bravely. Every step brought him nearer to London, farther from his own sober inartistic life. A light began to tremble on the horizon of his mind. He was not so old—thirty-two. His temperament might be said to be just at the point of maturity. There were so many different moods and impressions that he wished to express in verse. He felt them within him. He tried to weigh his soul to see if it was a poet's soul. Melancholy was the dominant note of his temperament, he thought, but it was a melancholy tempered by recurrences of faith and resignation and simple joy. If he could give expression to it in a book of poems perhaps men would listen. He would never be popular: he saw that. He could not sway the crowd but he might appeal to a little circle of kindred minds. The English critics perhaps would recognise him as one of the Celtic school by reason of the melancholy tone of his poems; besides that, he would put in allusions. He began to invent sentences and phrases from the notices which his book would get. *Mr. Chandler has the gift of easy and graceful verse....* *A wistful sadness pervades these poems.... The Celtic note.*[1] It was a pity his name was not more Irish looking. Perhaps it would be better to insert his mother's name before the surname: Thomas Malone Chandler, or better still: T. Malone Chandler. He would speak to Gallaher about it.

He pursued his revery so ardently that he passed his street and had to turn back. As he came near Corless's his former agitation began to overmaster him and he halted before the door in indecision. Finally he opened the door and entered.

The light and noise of the bar held him at the doorway for a few moments. He looked about him but his sight was confused by the shining of many red and green wineglasses. The bar seemed to him to be full of people and he felt that the people were observing him

---

1   *The Celtic note*   The Celtic Revival, also known as the Celtic Twilight, romanticized Irish culture by focusing on Celtic mythology, peasantry, and mysticism. Many of its most celebrated writers were Anglo-Irish rather than Celtic, and the movement bolstered English stereotypes of the Irish popularized by the English poet and critic Matthew Arnold in his *Study of Celtic Literature* (1867).

curiously. He glanced quickly to right and left (frowning slightly to make his errand appear serious) but when his sight cleared a little he saw that nobody had turned to look at him: and there, sure enough, was Ignatius Gallaher leaning with his back against the counter and his feet planted far apart.

—Hello, Tommy, old hero, here you are! What is it to be? What will you have? I'm taking whisky: better stuff than we get across the water. Soda? Lithia?[1] No mineral? I'm the same. Spoils the flavour.... Here, *garçon*, bring us two halves of malt whisky like a good fellow.... Well, and how have you been pulling along since I saw you last? Dear God, how old we're getting! Do you see any signs of aging in me—eh, what? A little grey and thin on the top—what?

Ignatius Gallaher took off his hat and displayed a large closely cropped head. His face was heavy, pale and cleanshaven. His eyes, which were of bluish slate colour, relieved his unhealthy pallor and shone out plainly above the vivid orange tie he wore. Between these rival features the lips appeared very long and shapeless and colourless. He bent his head and felt with two sympathetic fingers the thin hair at the crown. Little Chandler shook his head as a denial. Ignatius Gallaher put on his hat again.

—It pulls you down, he said, press life. Always hurry and scurry, looking for copy and sometimes not finding it: and then always to have something new in your stuff. Damn proofs and printers, I say, for a few days. I'm deuced glad, I can tell you, to get back to the old country. Does a fellow good, a bit of a holiday. I feel a ton better since I landed again in dear dirty Dublin[2] ... Here you are, Tommy. Water? Say when.

Little Chandler allowed his whisky to be very much diluted.

—You don't know what's good for you, my boy, said Ignatius Gallaher. I drink mine neat.

—I drink very little as a rule, said Little Chandler modestly. An odd half one or so when I meet any of the old crowd: that's all.

—Ah well, said Ignatius Gallaher cheerfully, here's to us and to old times and old acquaintance.

---

1 *Lithia* Bottled mineral water.

2 *dear dirty Dublin* Affectionate nickname made popular by Lady Morgan's novel *The Wild Irish Girl* (1806).

They clinked glasses and drank the toast.

—I met some of the old gang today, said Ignatius Gallaher. O'Hara seems to be in a bad way. What's he doing?

—Nothing, said Little Chandler. He's gone to the dogs.

—But Hogan has a good sit,[1] hasn't he?

—Yes; he's in the Land Commission.[2]

—I met him one night in London and he seemed to be very flush....[3] Poor O'Hara! Booze, I suppose?

—Other things, too, said Little Chandler shortly.

Ignatius Gallaher laughed.

—Tommy, he said, I see you haven't changed an atom. You're the very same serious person that used to lecture me on Sunday mornings when I had a sore head and a fur on my tongue. You'd want to knock about a bit in the world. Have you never been anywhere, even for a trip?

—I've been to the Isle of Man,[4] said Little Chandler.

Ignatius Gallaher laughed.

—The Isle of Man! he said. Go to London or Paris: Paris, for choice. That'd do you good.

—Have you seen Paris?

—I should think I have! I've knocked about there a little.

—And is it really so beautiful as they say? asked Little Chandler.

He sipped a little of his drink while Ignatius Gallaher finished his boldly.

—Beautiful? said Ignatius Gallaher, pausing on the word and on the flavour of his drink. It's not so beautiful, you know. Of course, it is beautiful.... But it's the life of Paris: that's the thing. Ah, there's no city like Paris for gaiety, movement, excitement....

Little Chandler finished his whisky and after some trouble succeeded in catching the barman's eye. He ordered the same again.

---

1 *a good sit* A good situation: secure employment.
2 *Land Commission* The Irish Land Commission Court, a British agency responsible for transferring farmland ownership from landlord to tenant (rectifying injustices of the 1880s, when Irish land had been confiscated by English and Scottish landlords).
3 *very flush* Supplied with a good deal of ready cash.
4 *Isle of Man* Island between England and Ireland. A mild climate makes it a popular resort.

—I've been to the Moulin Rouge,[1] Ignatius Gallaher continued when the barman had removed their glasses, and I've been to all the bohemian cafés. Hot stuff! Not for a pious chap like you, Tommy.

Little Chandler said nothing until the barman returned with the two glasses: then he touched his friend's glass lightly and reciprocated the former toast. He was beginning to feel somewhat disillusioned. Gallaher's accent and way of expressing himself did not please him. There was something vulgar in his friend which he had not observed before. But perhaps it was only the result of living in London amid the bustle and competition of the press. The old personal charm was still there under this new gaudy manner. And, after all, Gallaher had lived, he had seen the world. Little Chandler looked at his friend enviously.

—Everything in Paris is gay, said Ignatius Gallaher. They believe in enjoying life and don't you think they're right? If you want to enjoy yourself properly you must go to Paris. And, mind you, they've a great feeling for the Irish there. When they heard I was from Ireland they were ready to eat me, man.

Little Chandler took four or five sips from his glass.

—Tell me, he said, is it true that Paris is so … immoral as they say?

Ignatius Gallaher made a catholic[2] gesture with his right arm.

—Every place is immoral, he said. Of course you do find spicy bits in Paris. Go to one of the students' balls,[3] for instance. That's lively, if you like, when the *cocottes*[4] begin to let themselves loose. You know what they are, I suppose?

—I've heard of them, said Little Chandler.

Ignatius Gallaher drank off his whisky and shook his head.

—Ah, he said, you may say what you like. There's no woman like the Parisienne for style, for go.

—Then it is an immoral city, said Little Chandler with timid insistence, I mean, compared with London or Dublin?

---

1   *Moulin Rouge*   Famous Parisian cabaret.
2   *catholic*   Widespread, but also suggestive of the sign of the cross, which a devout Catholic might make at the mention of the "immoral[ity]" under discussion.
3   *students' balls*   Parties held in Parisian eating and drinking establishments and associated with the risqué.
4   *cocottes*   Slang: prostitutes.

—London! said Ignatius Gallaher. It's six of one and half a dozen of the other. You ask Hogan, my boy. I showed him a bit about London when he was over there. He'd open your eye.... I say, Tommy, don't make punch of that whisky: liquor up.

—No, really....

—O, come on, another one won't do you any harm. What is it? The same again, I suppose?

—Well ... all right.

—*François*, the same again.... Will you smoke, Tommy?

Ignatius Gallaher produced his cigar case. The two friends lit their cigars and puffed at them in silence until their drinks were served.

—I'll tell you my opinion, said Ignatius Gallaher, emerging after some time from the clouds of smoke in which he had taken refuge, it's a rum world. Talk of immorality! I've heard of cases—what am I saying—I've known them: cases of ... immorality ....

Ignatius Gallaher puffed thoughtfully at his cigar and then, in a calm historian's tone, he proceeded to sketch for his friend some pictures of the corruption which was rife abroad. He summarised the vices of many capitals and seemed inclined to award the palm to Berlin. Some things he could not vouch for (his friends had told him) but of others he had had personal experience. He spared neither rank nor caste. He revealed many of the secrets of religious houses on the continent and described some of the practices which were fashionable in high society: and ended by telling, with details, a story about an English duchess[1]—a story which he knew to be true. Little Chandler was astonished.

—Ah, well, said Ignatius Gallaher, here we are in old jogalong Dublin where nothing is known of such things.

—How dull you must find it, said Little Chandler, after all the other places you've seen!

—Well, said Ignatius Gallaher, it's a relaxation to come over here, you know. And, after all, it's the old country, as they say, isn't it? You can't help having a certain feeling for it. That's human nature.... But

---

1   *the secrets ... the continent*   Convents and monasteries had long been associated in English discourse (including pornography) with sexual deviance;   *a story about an English duchess*   The English aristocracy was likewise associated with licentiousness.

tell me something about yourself. Hogan told me you had … tasted the joys of connubial bliss. Two years ago, wasn't it?

Little Chandler blushed and smiled.

—Yes, he said. I was married last May twelve months.

—I hope it's not too late in the day to offer my best wishes, said Ignatius Gallaher. I didn't know your address or I'd have done so at the time.

He extended his hand which Little Chandler took.

—Well, Tommy, he said, I wish you and yours every joy in life, old chap, and tons of money and may you never die till I shoot you. And that's the wish of a sincere friend, an old friend. You know that?

—I know that, said Little Chandler.

—Any youngsters? said Ignatius Gallaher.

Little Chandler blushed again.

—We have one child, he said.

—Son or daughter?

—A little boy.

Ignatius Gallaher slapped his friend sonorously on the back.

—Bravo, he said, I wouldn't doubt you, Tommy.

Little Chandler smiled, looked confusedly at his glass and bit his lower lip with three childishly white front teeth.

—I hope you'll spend an evening with us, he said, before you go back. My wife will be delighted to meet you. We can have a little music and …

—Thanks awfully, old chap, said Ignatius Gallaher, I'm sorry we didn't meet earlier. But I must leave tomorrow night.

—Tonight, perhaps….

—I'm awfully sorry, old man. You see I'm over here with another fellow, clever young chap he is too, and we arranged to go to a little card party. Only for that ….

—O, in that case….

—But who knows? said Ignatius Gallaher considerately. Next year I may take a little skip over here now that I've broken the ice. It's only a pleasure deferred.

—Very well, said Little Chandler, the next time you come we must have an evening together. That's agreed now, isn't it?

—Yes, that's agreed, said Ignatius Gallaher. Next year if I come, *parole d'honneur*.[1]

—And to clinch the bargain, said Little Chandler, we'll just have one more now.

Ignatius Gallaher took out a large gold watch and looked at it.

—Is it to be the last? he said. Because, you know, I have an a.p.[2]

—O yes, positively, said Little Chandler.

—Very well then, said Ignatius Gallaher, let us have another one as a *deoc an doruis*[3]—that's good vernacular for a small whisky, I believe.

Little Chandler ordered the drinks. The blush which had risen to his face a few moments before was establishing itself. A trifle made him blush at any time: and now he felt warm and excited. Three small whiskies had gone to his head and Gallaher's strong cigar had confused his mind for he was a delicate and abstinent person. The adventure of meeting Gallaher after eight years, of finding himself with Gallaher in Corless's surrounded by lights and noise, of listening to Gallaher's stories and of sharing for a brief space Gallaher's vagrant and triumphant life, upset the equipoise of his sensitive nature. He felt acutely the contrast between his own life and his friend's and it seemed to him unjust. Gallaher was his inferior in birth and education. He was sure that he could do something better than his friend had ever done, or could ever do, something higher than mere tawdry journalism if he only got the chance. What was it that stood in his way? His unfortunate timidity! He wished to vindicate himself in some way, to assert his manhood. He saw behind Gallaher's refusal of his invitation. Gallaher was only patronising him by his friendliness just as he was patronising Ireland by his visit.

The barman brought their drinks. Little Chandler pushed one glass towards his friend and took up the other boldly.

—Who knows? he said as they lifted their glasses. When you come next year I may have the pleasure of wishing long life and happiness to Mr. and Mrs. Ignatius Gallaher.

---

1   *parole d'honneur*   French: word of honor.
2   *a.p.*   Probably slang for "appointment."
3   *deoc an doruis*   Irish: drink of the door; an expression equivalent to "one for the road."

Ignatius Gallaher in the act of drinking closed one eye expressively over the rim of his glass. When he had drunk he smacked his lips decisively, set down his glass and said:

—No blooming fear of that, my boy. I'm going to have my fling first and see a bit of life and the world before I put my head in the sack—if I ever do.

—Some day you will, said Little Chandler calmly.

Ignatius Gallaher turned his orange tie and slateblue eyes full upon his friend.

—You think so? he said.

—You'll put your head in the sack, repeated Little Chandler stoutly, like everyone else, if you can find the girl.

He had slightly emphasised his tone and he was aware that he had betrayed himself; but though the colour had heightened in his cheek he did not flinch from his friend's gaze. Ignatius Gallaher watched him for a few moments and then said:

—If ever it occurs you may bet your bottom dollar there'll be no mooning and spooning about it. I mean to marry money. She'll have a good fat account at the bank or she won't do for me.

Little Chandler shook his head.

—Why, man alive, said Ignatius Gallaher vehemently, do you know what it is? I've only to say the word and tomorrow I can have the woman and the cash. You don't believe it? Well, I know it. There are hundreds—what am I saying?—thousands of rich Germans and Jews, rotten with money, that'd only be too glad.... You wait awhile, my boy. See if I don't play my cards properly. When I go about a thing I mean business, I tell you. You just wait.

He tossed his glass to his mouth, finished his drink and laughed loudly. Then he looked thoughtfully before him and said in a calmer tone:

—But I'm in no hurry. They can wait. I don't fancy tying myself up to one woman, you know.

He imitated with his mouth the act of tasting and made a wry face.

—Must get a bit stale, I should think, he said.

*   *   *

Little Chandler sat in the room off the hall, holding a child in his arms. To save money they kept no servant but Annie's young sister

Monica came for an hour or so in the morning and an hour or so in the evening to help. But Monica had gone home long ago. It was a quarter to nine. Little Chandler had come home late for tea and, moreover, he had forgotten to bring Annie home the parcel of coffee from Bewley's.[1] Of course she was in a bad humour and gave him short answers. She said she would do without any tea but when it came near the time at which the shop at the corner closed she decided to go out herself for a quarter of a pound of tea and two pounds of sugar. She put the sleeping child deftly in his arms and said:

—Here. Don't waken him.

A little lamp with a white china shade stood upon the table and its light fell over a photograph which was enclosed in a frame of crumpled horn. It was Annie's photograph. Little Chandler looked at it, pausing at the thin tight lips. She wore the pale blue summer blouse which he had brought her home as a present one Saturday. It had cost him ten and elevenpence;[2] but what an agony of nervousness it had cost him! How he had suffered that day, waiting at the shopdoor until the shop was empty, standing at the counter and trying to appear at his ease while the girl piled ladies' blouses before him, paying at the desk and forgetting to take up the odd penny of his change, being called back by the cashier and, finally, striving to hide his blushes as he left the shop by examining the parcel to see if it was securely tied. When he brought the blouse home Annie kissed him and said it was very pretty and stylish but when she heard the price she threw the blouse on the table and said it was a regular swindle to charge ten and elevenpence for that. At first she wanted to take it back but when she tried it on she was delighted with it, especially with the make of the sleeves, and kissed him and said he was very good to think of her.

Hm!...

He looked coldly into the eyes of the photograph and they answered coldly. Certainly they were pretty and the face itself was pretty. But he found something mean in it. Why was it so uncon-

---

1 *Bewley's* One of a chain of tea and coffee shops in Dublin.
2 *ten and elevenpence* Ten shillings and eleven pence, a high price relative to Chandler's income.

scious and ladylike? The composure of the eyes irritated him. They repelled him and defied him: there was no passion in them, no rapture. He thought of what Gallaher had said about rich Jewesses. Those dark oriental eyes, he thought, how full they are of passion, of voluptuous longing!...[1] Why had he married the eyes in the photograph?

He caught himself up at the question and glanced nervously round the room. He found something mean in the pretty furniture which he had bought for his house on the hire system.[2] Annie had chosen it herself and it reminded him of her. It too was prim and pretty. A dull resentment against his life awoke within him. Could he not escape from his little house? Was it too late for him to try to live bravely like Gallaher? Could he go to London? There was the furniture still to be paid for. If he could only write a book and get it published, that might open the way for him.

A volume of Byron's[3] poems lay before him on the table. He opened it cautiously with his left hand lest he should waken the child and began to read the first poem in the book:

> *Hushed are the winds and still the evening gloom,*
> *Not e'en a Zephyr wanders through the grove,*
> *Whilst I return to view my Margaret's tomb*
> *And scatter flowers on the dust I love.*[4]

He paused. He felt the rhythm of the verse about him in the room. How melancholy it was! Could he, too, write like that, express the melancholy of his soul in verse? There were so many things he wanted to describe: his sensation of a few hours before on Grattan Bridge, for example. If he could get back again into that mood....

---

1   *rich Jewesses ... longing*   An example of both anti-Semitism and Orientalism, associating Jews with the East, and both Jews and Easterners with sensuality specifically and a lack of restraint more broadly. For more on Orientalism, see the introduction, page 12.

2   *on the hire system*   On credit.

3   *Byron*   George Gordon, Lord Byron (1788–1824), an English Romantic poet.

4   *Hushed are ... I love*   First stanza of Byron's poem "On the Death of a Young Lady, Cousin of the Author, and Very Dear to Him," written in 1802, published in *Hours of Idleness* (1807).

The child awoke and began to cry. He turned from the page and tried to hush it: but it would not be hushed. He began to rock it to and fro in his arms but its wailing cry grew keener. He rocked it faster while his eyes began to read the second stanza:

> *Within this narrow cell reclines her clay,*
> *That clay where once ...*

It was useless. He couldn't read. He couldn't do anything. The wailing of the child pierced the drum of his ear. It was useless, useless! He was a prisoner for life. His arms trembled with anger and suddenly bending to the child's face he shouted:

—Stop!

The child stopped for an instant, had a spasm of fright and began to scream. He jumped up from his chair and walked hastily up and down the room with the child in his arms. It began to sob piteously, losing its breath for four or five seconds and then bursting out anew. The thin walls of the room echoed the sound. He tried to soothe it but it sobbed more convulsively. He looked at the contracted and quivering face of the child and began to be alarmed. He counted seven sobs without a break between them and caught the child to his breast in fright. If it died!...

The door was burst open and a young woman ran in, panting.

—What is it? What is it? she cried.

The child, hearing its mother's voice, broke out into a paroxysm of sobbing.

—It's nothing, Annie ... it's nothing.... He began to cry....

She flung her parcels on the floor and snatched the child from him.

—What have you done to him? she cried, glaring into his face.

Little Chandler sustained for one moment the gaze of her eyes and his heart closed together as he met the hatred in them. He began to stammer:

—It's nothing.... He ... he began to cry.... I couldn't ... I didn't do anything.... What?

Giving no heed to him she began to walk up and down the room, clasping the child tightly in her arms and murmuring:

—My little man! My little mannie! Was 'ou frightened, love?…
There now, love! There now!… Lambabaun![1] Mamma's little lamb of
the world!… There now!

Little Chandler felt his cheeks suffused with shame and he stood
back out of the lamplight. He listened while the paroxysm of the
child's sobbing grew less and less: and tears of remorse started to his
eyes.

---

1 *Lambabaun*   Irish term of endearment meaning "lamb child."

Interior of a Dublin pub, c. 1910. This image shows the bar of a pub similar to the one in which Little Chandler and Ignatius Gallaher drink whisky in "A Little Cloud."

The Dead

Lily, the caretaker's daughter, was literally run off her feet. Hardly had she brought one gentleman into the little pantry behind the office on the groundfloor and helped him off with his overcoat when the wheezy halldoor bell clanged again and she had to scamper along the bare hallway to let in another guest. It was well for her she had not to attend to the ladies also. But Miss Kate and Miss Julia had thought of that and had converted the bathroom upstairs into a ladies' dressing-room. Miss Kate and Miss Julia were there, gossiping and laughing and fussing, walking after each other to the head of the stairs, peering down over the banisters and calling down to Lily to ask her who had come.

It was always a great affair, the Misses Morkan's annual dance. Everybody who knew them came to it, members of the family, old friends of the family, the members of Julia's choir, any of Kate's pupils that were grown up enough and even some of Mary Jane's pupils too. Never once had it fallen flat. For years and years it had gone off in splendid style as long as anyone could remember, ever since Kate and Julia, after the death of their brother Pat, had left the house in Stony Batter and taken Mary Jane, their only niece, to live with them in the dark gaunt house on Usher's Island, the upper part of which they had rented from Mr. Fullam, the corn factor[1] on the groundfloor. That was a good thirty years ago if it was a day. Mary Jane, who was then a little girl in short clothes, was now the main prop of the household for she had the organ in Haddington Road. She had been through the academy[2] and gave a pupils' concert every year in the upper room of the Antient Concert Rooms. Many of her pupils belonged to better class families on the Kingstown and Dalkey line. Old as they were, her aunts also did their share. Julia, though she was quite grey, was still the leading soprano in Adam and Eve's[3] and Kate, being too feeble to go about much, gave music lessons to beginners on the old square piano in the back room. Lily, the caretaker's daughter, did housemaid

---

1   *corn factor*   Grain merchant.
2   *the academy*   Royal Irish Academy of Music.
3   *Adam and Eve's*   Familiar name of Dublin's Church of the Immaculate Conception.

work for them. Though their life was modest they believed in eating well, the best of everything: diamond bone sirloins, three shilling tea and the best bottled stout. But Lily seldom made a mistake in the orders so that she got on well with her three mistresses. They were fussy, that was all. But the only thing they would not stand was back answers.[1]

Of course they had good reason to be fussy on such a night. And then it was long after ten o'clock and yet there was no sign of Gabriel and his wife. Besides they were dreadfully afraid that Freddy Malins might turn up screwed.[2] They would not wish for worlds that any of Mary Jane's pupils should see him under the influence: and when he was like that it was sometimes very hard to manage him. Freddy Malins always came late but they wondered what could be keeping Gabriel: and that was what brought them every two minutes to the banisters to ask Lily had Gabriel or Freddy come.

—O, Mr. Conroy, said Lily to Gabriel when she opened the door for him, Miss Kate and Miss Julia thought you were never coming. Good night, Mrs. Conroy.

—I'll engage they did, said Gabriel, but they forget that my wife here takes three mortal hours to dress herself.

He stood on the mat, scraping the snow from his goloshes, while Lily led his wife to the foot of the stairs and called out:

—Miss Kate, here's Mrs. Conroy.

Kate and Julia came toddling down the dark stairs at once. Both of them kissed Gabriel's wife, said she must be perished alive and asked was Gabriel with her.

—Here I am as right as the mail, aunt Kate! Go on up. I'll follow, called out Gabriel from the dark.

He continued scraping his feet vigorously while the three women went upstairs, laughing, to the ladies' dressingroom. A light fringe of snow lay like a cape on the shoulders of his overcoat and like toecaps on the toes of his goloshes; and, as the buttons of his overcoat slipped with a squeaking noise through the snowstiffened frieze,[3] a cold fragrant air from out of doors escaped from crevices and folds.

—Is it snowing again, Mr. Conroy? asked Lily.

---

1 *back answers* Back-talk.
2 *screwed* Drunk.
3 *frieze* Coarse woolen cloth.

She had preceded him into the pantry to help him off with his overcoat. Gabriel smiled at the three syllables she had given his surname and glanced at her. She was a slim growing girl, pale in complexion and with haycoloured hair. The gas in the pantry made her look still paler. Gabriel had known her when she was a child and used to sit on the lowest step nursing a rag doll.

—Yes, Lily, he answered, and I think we're in for a night of it.

He looked up at the pantry ceiling which was shaking with the stamping and shuffling of feet on the floor above, listened for a moment to the piano and then glanced at the girl who was folding his overcoat carefully at the end of a shelf.

—Tell me, Lily, he said in a friendly tone, do you still go to school?

—O no, sir, she answered, I'm done schooling this year and more.

—O then, said Gabriel gaily, I suppose we'll be going to your wedding one of these fine days with your young man—eh?

The girl glanced back at him over her shoulder and said with great bitterness:

—The men that is now is only all palaver and what they can get out of you.

Gabriel coloured as if he felt he had made a mistake and, without looking at her, kicked off his goloshes and flicked actively with his muffler at his patent leather shoes.

He was a stout tallish young man. The high colour of his cheeks pushed upwards even to his forehead where it scattered itself in a few formless patches of pale red; and on his hairless face there scintillated restlessly the polished lenses and bright gilt rims of the glasses which screened his delicate and restless eyes. His glossy black hair was parted in the middle and brushed in a long curve behind his ears where it curled slightly beneath the groove left by his hat.

When he had flicked lustre into his shoes he stood up and pulled his waistcoat down more tightly on his plump body. Then he took a coin rapidly from his pocket.

—O Lily, he said, thrusting it into her hand, it's Christmas time, isn't it? Just .... here's a little ....

He walked rapidly towards the door.

—O no, sir! cried the girl, following him. Really, sir, I wouldn't take it.

—Christmas time! Christmas time! said Gabriel, almost trotting to the stairs and waving his hand to her in deprecation.

The girl, seeing that he had gained the stairs, called out after him:

—Well, thank you, sir.

He waited outside the drawingroom door until the waltz should finish, listening to the skirts that swept against it and to the shuffling of feet. He was still discomposed by the girl's bitter and sudden retort. It had cast a gloom over him which he tried to dispel by arranging his cuffs and the bows of his tie. Then he took from his waistcoat pocket a little paper and glanced at the headings he had made for his speech. He was undecided about the lines from Robert Browning[1] for he feared they would be above the heads of his hearers. Some quotation that they could recognise from Shakespeare or from the melodies[2] would be better. The indelicate clacking of the men's heels and the shuffling of their soles reminded him that their grade of culture differed from his. He would only make himself ridiculous by quoting poetry to them which they could not understand. They would think that he was airing his superior education. He would fail with them just as he had failed with the girl in the pantry. He had taken up a wrong tone. His whole speech was a mistake from first to last, an utter failure.

Just then his aunts and his wife came out of the ladies' dressingroom. His aunts were two small plainly dressed old women. Aunt Julia was an inch or so the taller. Her hair, drawn low over the tops of her ears, was grey; and grey also, with darker shadows, was her large flaccid face. Though she was stout in build and stood erect her slow eyes and parted lips gave her the appearance of a woman who did not know where she was or where she was going. Aunt Kate was more vivacious. Her face, healthier than her sister's, was all puckers and creases like a shrivelled red apple and her hair, braided in the same oldfashioned way, had not lost its ripe nut colour.

They both kissed Gabriel frankly. He was their favourite nephew, the son of their dead elder sister Ellen who had married T.J. Conroy of the Port and Docks.[3]

---

1 *Robert Browning* English poet (1812–89).

2 *melodies* *Irish Melodies* (1807–34), by Irish poet Thomas Moore, was a ten-volume collection of poems written to accompany well-known Irish tunes.

3 *Port and Docks* Dublin Port and Docks Board, an essential part of Dublin's commercial life.

—Gretta tells me you're not going to take a cab back to Monkstown tonight, Gabriel, said aunt Kate.

—No, said Gabriel, turning to his wife, we had quite enough of that last year, hadn't we? Don't you remember, aunt Kate, what a cold Gretta got out of it? Cab windows rattling all the way and the east wind blowing in after we passed Merrion. Very jolly it was. Gretta caught a dreadful cold.

Aunt Kate frowned severely and nodded her head at every word.

—Quite right, Gabriel, quite right, she said. You can't be too careful.

—But as for Gretta there, said Gabriel, she'd walk home in the snow if she were let.

Mrs. Conroy laughed.

—Don't mind him, aunt Kate, she said. He's really an awful bother, what with green shades for Tom's eyes at night and making him do the dumbbells and forcing Lottie to eat the stirabout.[1] The poor child! And she simply hates the sight of it!.... O, but you'll never guess what he makes me wear now!

She broke out into a peal of laughter and glanced at her husband whose admiring and happy eyes had been wandering from her dress to her face and hair. The two aunts laughed heartily too for Gabriel's solicitude was a standing joke with them.

—Goloshes! said Mrs. Conroy. That's the latest. Whenever it's wet underfoot I must put on my goloshes. Tonight even he wanted me to put them on but I wouldn't. The next thing he'll buy me will be a diving suit.

Gabriel laughed nervously and patted his tie reassuringly while aunt Kate nearly doubled herself so heartily did she enjoy the joke. The smile soon faded from aunt Julia's face and her mirthless eyes were directed towards her nephew's face. After a pause she asked:

—And what are goloshes, Gabriel?

—Goloshes, Julia! exclaimed her sister. Goodness me, don't you know what goloshes are? You wear them over your .... over your boots, Gretta, isn't it?

—Yes, said Mrs. Conroy. Guttapercha[2] things. We both have a pair now. Gabriel says everyone wears them on the continent.

---

1 *stirabout* Porridge.

2 *Guttapercha* Substance similar to rubber and used for waterproofing.

—O, on the continent, murmured aunt Julia, nodding her head slowly.

Gabriel knitted his brows and said, as if he were slightly angered:

—It's nothing very wonderful but Gretta thinks it very funny because she says the word reminds her of christy minstrels.[1]

—But tell me, Gabriel, said aunt Kate with brisk tact. Of course you've seen about the room. Gretta was saying ....

—O, the room is all right, replied Gabriel. I've taken one in the Gresham.[2]

—To be sure, said aunt Kate, by far the best thing to do. And the children, Gretta, you're not anxious about them?

—O, for one night, said Mrs. Conroy. Besides Bessie will look after them.

—To be sure, said aunt Kate again. What a comfort it is to have a girl like that, one you can depend on! There's that Lily, I'm sure I don't know what has come over her lately. She's not the girl she was at all.

Gabriel was about to ask his aunt some questions on this point but she broke off suddenly to gaze after her sister who had wandered down the stairs and was craning her neck over the banisters.

—Now, I ask you, she said almost testily, where is Julia going. Julia! Julia! Where are you going?

Julia who had gone half way down one flight came back and announced blandly:

—Here's Freddy!

At the same moment a clapping of hands and a final flourish of the pianist told that the waltz had ended. The drawingroom door was opened from within and some couples came out. Aunt Kate drew Gabriel aside hurriedly and whispered into his ear:

—Slip down, Gabriel, like a good fellow and see if he's all right and don't let him up if he's screwed. I'm sure he's screwed. I'm sure he is.

---

1 *christy minstrels* Theatrical entertainment commonly associated with blackface. John Wyse Jackson and Bernard McGinley speculate that Gretta is reminded of the minstrels by galoshes, because with her Galway accent she would pronounce the word as "golly shoes," which sounds like "golliwogg." Based on a character from a series of children's books, dressed in minstrel clothes, jet black, and grinning widely, the racist image of the golliwogg (often as a ragdoll) circulated widely from the end of the nineteenth through the middle of the twentieth century.

2 *Gresham* One of Dublin's top hotels.

Gabriel went to the stairs and listened over the banisters. He could hear two persons talking in the pantry. Then he recognised Freddy Malins' laugh. He went down the stairs noisily.

—It's such a relief, said aunt Kate to Mrs. Conroy, that Gabriel is here. I always feel easier in my mind when he's here ..... Julia, there's Miss Daly and Miss Power will take some refreshment. Thanks for your beautiful waltz, Miss Daly. It made lovely time.

A tall wizenfaced man with a stiff grizzled moustache and swarthy skin who was passing out with his partner said:

—And may we have some refreshment too, Miss Morkan?

—Julia, said aunt Kate summarily, and here's Mr. Browne and Miss Furlong. Take them in, Julia, with Miss Daly and Miss Power.

—I'm the man for the ladies, said Mr. Browne, pursing his lips until his moustache bristled and smiling in all his wrinkles. You know, Miss Morkan, the reason they are so fond of me is .....

He did not finish his sentence but, seeing that aunt Kate was out of earshot, at once led the three young ladies into the back room. The middle of the room was occupied by two square tables placed end to end and on these aunt Julia and the caretaker were straightening and smoothing a large cloth. On the sideboard were arrayed dishes and plates and glasses and bundles of knives and forks and spoons. The top of the closed square piano served also as a sideboard for viands and sweets. At a smaller sideboard in one corner two young men were standing, drinking hop bitters.

Mr. Browne led his charges thither and invited them all, in jest, to some ladies' punch, hot, strong and sweet. As they said they never took anything strong he opened three bottles of lemonade for them. Then he asked one of the young men to move aside and, taking hold of the decanter, filled out for himself a goodly measure of whisky. The young men eyed him respectfully while he took a trial sip.

—God help me, he said smiling, it's the doctor's orders.

His wizened face broke into a broader smile and the three young ladies laughed in musical echo to his pleasantry, swaying their bodies to and fro, with nervous jerks of their shoulders. The boldest said:

—O, now, Mr. Browne, I'm sure the doctor never ordered anything of the kind.

Mr. Browne took another sip of his whisky and said, with sidling mimicry:

—Well, you see, I'm like the famous Mrs. Cassidy who is reported to have said: *Now, Mary Grimes, if I don't take it make me take it for I feel I want it.*[1]

His hot face had leaned forward a little too confidentially and he had assumed a very low Dublin accent so that the young ladies, with one instinct, received his speech in silence. Miss Furlong, who was one of Mary Jane's pupils, asked Miss Daly what was the name of the pretty waltz she had played; and Mr. Browne, seeing that he was ignored, turned promptly to the two young men who were more appreciative.

A redfaced young woman, dressed in pansy, came into the room, excitedly clapping her hands and crying:

—Quadrilles![2] Quadrilles!

Close on her heels came aunt Kate, crying:

—Two gentlemen and three ladies, Mary Jane!

—O, here's Mr. Bergin and Mr. Kerrigan, said Mary Jane. Mr. Kerrigan, will you take Miss Power. Miss Furlong, may I get you a partner, Mr. Bergin. O, that'll just do now.

—Three ladies, Mary Jane, said aunt Kate.

The two young gentlemen asked the ladies if they might have the pleasure and Mary Jane turned to Miss Daly.

—O, Miss Daly, you're really awfully good after playing for the last two dances but really we're so short of ladies tonight.

—I don't mind in the least, Miss Morkan.

—But I've a nice partner for you, Mr. Bartell D'Arcy, the tenor. I'll get him to sing later on. All Dublin is raving about him.

—Lovely voice, lovely voice! said aunt Kate.

As the piano had twice begun the prelude to the first figure Mary Jane led her recruits quickly from the room. They had hardly gone when aunt Julia wandered slowly into the room, looking behind her at something.

—What is the matter, Julia? asked aunt Kate anxiously. Who is it?

---

1   *Mrs. Cassidy … I feel I want it*   The origin of this statement is unknown, but it appears to be a joke suggesting the baseness of women.

2   *Quadrilles*   Type of square dance that originated in France.

Julia, who was carrying in a column of table-napkins, turned to her sister and said simply, as if the question had surprised her:

—It's only Freddy, Kate, and Gabriel with him.

In fact right behind her Gabriel could be seen piloting Freddy Malins across the landing. The latter, a young man of about forty, was of Gabriel's size and build with very round shoulders. His face was fleshy and pallid, touched with colour only at the thick hanging lobes of his ears and at the wide wings of his nose. He had coarse features, a blunt nose, a convex and receding brow, tumid and protruded lips. His heavylidded eyes and the disorder of his scanty hair made him look sleepy. He was laughing heartily in a high key at a story which he had been telling Gabriel on the stairs and at the same time rubbing the knuckles of his left fist backwards and forwards into his left eye.

—Good evening, Freddy, said aunt Julia.

Freddy Malins bade the Misses Morkan good evening in what seemed an offhand fashion by reason of the habitual catch in his voice and then, seeing that Mr. Browne was grinning at him from the sideboard, crossed the room on rather shaky legs and began to repeat in an undertone the story he had just told to Gabriel.

—He's not so bad, is he? said aunt Kate to Gabriel.

Gabriel's brows were dark but he raised them quickly and answered:

—O no, hardly noticeable.

—Now, isn't he a terrible fellow! she said. And his poor mother made him take the pledge[1] on New Year's Eve. But come on, Gabriel, into the drawingroom.

Before leaving the room with Gabriel she signalled to Mr. Browne by frowning and shaking her forefinger in warning to and fro. Mr. Browne nodded in answer and, when she had gone, said to Freddy Malins:

—Now then, Teddy, I'm going to fill you out a good glass of lemonade just to buck you up.

Freddy Malins, who was nearing the climax of his story, waved the offer aside impatiently but Mr. Browne, having first called Freddy Malins' attention to a disarray in his dress, filled out and handed him a full glass of lemonade. Freddy Malins' left hand accepted the glass mechanically, his right hand being engaged in the mechanical

---

1   *take the pledge*   I.e., pledge to abstain from alcoholic beverages.

readjustment of his dress. Mr. Browne, whose face was once more wrinkling with mirth, poured out for himself a glass of whisky while Freddy Malins exploded, before he had well reached the climax of his story, in a kink of highpitched bronchitic laughter and, setting down his untasted and overflowing glass, began to rub the knuckles of his left fist backwards and forwards into his left eye, repeating words of his last phrase as well as his fit of laughter would allow him.

*　　*　　*

Gabriel could not listen while Mary Jane was playing her academy piece, full of runs and difficult passages, to the hushed drawingroom. He liked music but the piece she was playing had no melody for him and he doubted whether it had any melody for the other listeners though they had begged Mary Jane to play something. Four young men, who had come from the refreshment room to stand in the doorway at the sound of the piano, had gone away quietly in couples after a few minutes. The only persons who seemed to follow the music were Mary Jane herself, her hands racing along the keyboard or lifted from it at the pauses like those of a priestess in momentary imprecation, and aunt Kate standing at her elbow to turn the page.

Gabriel's eyes, irritated by the floor which glittered with beeswax under the heavy chandelier, wandered to the wall above the piano. A picture of the balcony scene in *Romeo and Juliet* hung there and beside it was a picture of the two murdered princes in the tower[1] which aunt Julia had worked in red, blue and brown wools when she was a girl. Probably in the school they had gone to as girls that kind of work had been taught, for one year his mother had worked for him as a birthday present a waistcoat of purple tabinet with little foxes' heads upon it, lined with brown satin and having round mulberry buttons. It was strange that his mother had had no musical talent though aunt Kate used to call her the brainscarrier of the Morkan family. Both she and Julia had always seemed a little proud of their serious and matronly sister. Her photograph stood before the pierglass.[2] She held an open book on her knees and was pointing out something in it to Constantine who, dressed in a man-o'-war suit,[3] lay at her feet.

---

1 *the two ... tower* Edward IV's two sons were murdered in the Tower of London in about 1483–84, allegedly at the instigation of their uncle, the future Richard III.

2 *pierglass* Long mirror.

3 *man-o'-war suit* Sailor suit, commonly worn by children.

It was she who had chosen the names for her sons for she was very sensible of the dignity of family life. Thanks to her, Constantine was now senior curate in Balbriggan and, thanks to her, Gabriel himself had taken his degree in the royal university. A shadow passed over his face as he remembered her sullen opposition to his marriage. Some slighting phrases she had used still rankled in his memory. She had once spoken of Gretta as being country cute and that was not true of Gretta at all. It was Gretta who had nursed her all during her last long illness in their house at Monkstown.

He knew that Mary Jane must be near the end of her piece for she was playing again the opening melody with runs of scales after every bar and while he waited for the end the resentment died down in his heart. The piece ended with a trill of octaves in the treble and a final deep octave in the bass. Great applause greeted Mary Jane as, blushing and rolling up her music nervously, she escaped from the room. The most vigorous clapping came from the four young men in the doorway who had gone away to the refreshment room at the beginning of the piece but had come back when the piano had stopped.

Lancers[1] were arranged. Gabriel found himself partnered with Miss Ivors. She was a frankmannered talkative young lady with a freckled face and prominent brown eyes. She did not wear a lowcut bodice and the large brooch which was fixed in the front of her collar bore on it an Irish device.[2]

When they had taken their places she said abruptly:

—I have a crow to pluck with you.

—With me? said Gabriel.

She nodded her head gravely.

—What is it? asked Gabriel, smiling at her solemn manner.

—Who is G.C.? answered Miss Ivors turning her eyes upon him.

Gabriel coloured and was about to knit his brows as if he did not understand when she said bluntly:

—O, innocent Amy! I have found out that you write for the *Daily Express*.[3] Now aren't you ashamed of yourself?

—Why should I be ashamed of myself? asked Gabriel blinking his eyes and trying to smile.

---

1   *Lancers*   Type of quadrille.
2   *Irish device*   Celtic design.
3   *Daily Express*   Dublin newspaper that opposed Irish independence.

—Well, I'm ashamed of you, said Miss Ivors frankly. To say you'd write for a rag like that. I didn't think you were a west Briton.[1]

A look of perplexity appeared on Gabriel's face. It was true that he wrote a literary column every Wednesday in the *Daily Express* for which he was paid fifteen shillings. But that did not make him a west Briton surely. The books he received for review were almost more welcome than the paltry cheque. He loved to feel the covers and turn over the pages of newly printed books. Nearly every day when his teaching in the college was ended he used to wander down the quays to the secondhand booksellers, to Hickey's on Bachelor's Walk, to Webb's or Massey's on Aston's Quay or to Clohissey's in the bystreet. He did not know how to meet her charge. He wanted to say that literature was above politics. But they were friends of many years' standing and their careers had been parallel, first at the university and then as teachers: he could not risk a grandiose phrase with her. He continued blinking his eyes and trying to smile and murmured lamely that he saw nothing political in writing reviews of books.

When their turn to cross had come he was still perplexed and inattentive. Miss Ivors promptly took his hand in a warm grasp and said in a soft friendly tone:

—Of course, I was only joking. Come, we cross now.

When they were together again she spoke of the university question[2] and Gabriel felt more at ease. A friend of hers had shown her his review of Browning's poems. That was how she had found out the secret: but she liked the review immensely. Then she said suddenly:

—O, Mr. Conroy, will you come for an excursion to the Aran Isles[3] this summer? We're going to stay there a whole month. It will be splendid out in the Atlantic. You ought to come. Mr. Clancy is coming and Mr. Kilkelly and Kathleen Kearney. It would be splendid for Gretta too if she'd come. She's from Connacht,[4] isn't she?

—Her people are, said Gabriel shortly.

---

1 *west Briton* Derogatory term for an Anglicized Irish person.

2 *university question* Debate about how to provide Irish Catholics with a university education equal to that of the best English and Anglo-Irish institutions, in an Irish cultural climate.

3 *Aran Isles* Group of Islands off of Ireland's west coast that were well known for preserving the Irish language and Irish traditions.

4 *Connacht* Irish spelling of Connaught, in west Ireland.

—But you will come, won't you? said Miss Ivors, laying her warm hand eagerly on his arm.

—The fact is, said Gabriel, I have already arranged to go ...

—Go where? asked Miss Ivors.

—Well, you know, every year I go for a cycling tour with some fellows and so ...

—But where? asked Miss Ivors.

—Well, we usually go to France or Belgium or perhaps Germany, said Gabriel awkwardly.

—And why do you go to France and Belgium, said Miss Ivors, instead of visiting your own land?

—Well, said Gabriel, it's partly to keep in touch with the languages and partly for a change.

—And haven't you your own language to keep in touch with, Irish? asked Miss Ivors.

—Well, said Gabriel, if it comes to that, you know, Irish is not my language.

Their neighbours had turned to listen to the crossexamination. Gabriel glanced right and left nervously and tried to keep his good humour under the ordeal which was making a blush invade his forehead.

—And haven't you your own land to visit, continued Miss Ivors, that you know nothing of, your own people and your own country?

—O, to tell you the truth, retorted Gabriel suddenly, I'm sick of my own country, sick of it!

—Why? asked Miss Ivors.

Gabriel did not answer for his retort had heated him.

—Why? repeated Miss Ivors.

They had to go visiting[1] together and, as he had not answered her, Miss Ivors said warmly:

—Of course, you've no answer.

Gabriel tried to cover his agitation by taking part in the dance with great energy. He avoided her eyes for he had seen a sour expression on her face. But when they met in the long chain he was surprised to feel his hand firmly pressed. She looked at him from under her brows

---

1 *go visiting* Reference to the part of a dance in which the partners cross the floor together and meet other dancers.

for a moment quizzically until he smiled. Then, just as the chain was about to start again, she stood on tiptoe and whispered into his ear:

—West Briton!

When the lancers were over Gabriel went away to a remote corner of the room where Freddy Malins' mother was sitting. She was a stout feeble old woman with white hair. Her voice had a catch in it like her son's and she stuttered slightly. She had been told that Freddy had come and that he was nearly all right. Gabriel asked her whether she had had a good crossing. She lived with her married daughter in Glasgow and came to Dublin on a visit once a year. She answered placidly that she had had a beautiful crossing and that the captain had been most attentive to her. She spoke also of the beautiful house her daughter kept in Glasgow and of the nice friends they had there. While her tongue rambled on Gabriel tried to banish from his mind all memory of the unpleasant incident with Miss Ivors. Of course the girl or woman or whatever she was was an enthusiast but there was a time for all things. Perhaps he ought not to have answered her like that. But she had no right to call him a west Briton before people, even in joke. She had tried to make him ridiculous before people, heckling him and staring at him with her rabbit's eyes.

He saw his wife making her way towards him through the waltzing couples. When she reached him she said into his ear:

—Gabriel, aunt Kate wants to know won't you carve the goose as usual. Miss Daly will carve the ham and I'll do the pudding.

—All right, said Gabriel.

—She's sending in the younger ones first as soon as this waltz is over so that we'll have the table to ourselves.

—Were you dancing? asked Gabriel.

—Of course I was. Didn't you see me? What words had you with Molly Ivors?

—No words. Why! Did she say so?

—Something like that. I'm trying to get that Mr. D'Arcy to sing. He's full of conceit, I think.

—There were no words, said Gabriel moodily, only she wanted me to go for a trip to the west of Ireland and I said I wouldn't.

His wife clasped her hands excitedly and gave a little jump.

—O, do go, Gabriel, she cried. I'd love to see Galway again.

—You can go if you like, said Gabriel coldly.

She looked at him for a moment, then turned to Mrs. Malins and said:

—There's a nice husband for you, Mrs. Malins.

While she was threading her way back across the room Mrs. Malins, without adverting to the interruption, went on to tell Gabriel what beautiful places there were in Scotland and beautiful scenery. Her son-in-law brought them every year to the lakes and they used to go fishing. Her son-in-law was a splendid fisher. One day he caught a fish, a beautiful big big fish: and the man in the hotel boiled it for their dinner.

Gabriel hardly heard what she said. Now that supper was coming near he began to think again about his speech and about the quotation. When he saw Freddy Malins coming across the room to visit his mother Gabriel left the chair free for him and retired into the embrasure of the window. The room had already cleared and from the back room came the clatter of plates and knives. Those who still remained in the drawingroom seemed tired of dancing and were conversing quietly in little groups. Gabriel's warm trembling fingers tapped the cold pane of the window. How cool it must be outside! How pleasant it would be to walk out alone, first along by the river and then through the park! The snow would be lying on the branches of the trees and forming a bright cap on the top of the Wellington monument.[1] How much more pleasant it would be there than at the supper table!

He ran over the headings of his speech: Irish hospitality, sad memories, the Three Graces, Paris,[2] the quotation from Browning. He repeated to himself a phrase he had written in his review: *One feels that one is listening to a thoughttormented music*. Miss Ivors had praised the review. Was she sincere? Had she really any life of her own behind all her propagandism? There had never been any ill feeling between them until that night. It unnerved him to think that she would be at

---

1   *Wellington monument*   Monument to Arthur Wellesley, the 1st Duke of Wellington (1769–1852), a member of the Anglo-Irish ascendency (typically Protestant elite of English heritage) and a great military general.

2   *Three Graces*   In Greek mythology, three daughters of Zeus who embody beauty and charm;   *Paris*   In Greek mythology, Paris was tasked with choosing the most beautiful of three goddesses. His prize was Helen, the world's most beautiful human woman; in running off with her, he effectively brought about the Trojan War.

the supper table, looking up at him while he spoke with her critical quizzing eyes. Perhaps she would not be sorry to see him fail in his speech. An idea came into his mind and gave him courage. He would say, alluding to aunt Kate and aunt Julia: *Ladies and gentlemen, the generation which is now on the wane among us may have had its faults but for my part I think it had certain qualities of hospitality, of humour, of humanity, which the new and very serious and hypereducated generation that is growing up around us seems to me to lack.* Very good: that was one for Miss Ivors. What did he care that his aunts were only two ignorant old women?

A murmur in the room attracted his attention. Mr. Browne was advancing from the door, gallantly escorting aunt Julia who leaned upon his arm, smiling and hanging her head. An irregular musketry of applause escorted her also as far as the piano and then, as Mary Jane seated herself on the stool and aunt Julia, no longer smiling, half turned so as to pitch her voice fairly into the room, gradually ceased. Gabriel recognised the prelude. It was that of an old song of aunt Julia's, *Arrayed for the Bridal.*[1] Her voice strong and clear in tone attacked with great spirit the runs which embellish the air and, though she sang very rapidly, she did not miss even the smallest of the grace notes. To follow the voice, without looking at the singer's face, was to feel and share the excitement of swift and secure flight. Gabriel applauded loudly with all the others at the close of the song and loud applause was borne in from the invisible supper table. It sounded so genuine that a little colour struggled into aunt Julia's face as she bent to replace in the music stand the old leatherbound songbook that had her initials on the cover. Freddy Malins, who had listened with his head perched sideways to hear the better, was still applauding when everyone else had ceased and talking animatedly to his mother who nodded her head gravely and slowly in acquiescence. At last, when he could clap no more, he stood up suddenly and hurried across the room to aunt Julia, whose hand he seized and held in both his hands, shaking it when words failed him or the catch in his voice proved too much for him.

---

1 *Arrayed for the Bridal* English writer George Linley (1798–1865) wrote the lyrics to this song, which was set to music from *I Puritani*, an 1835 opera by Italian composer Vincenzo Bellini.

—I was just telling my mother, he said, I never heard you sing so well, never. No, I never heard your voice so good as it is tonight. Now! Would you believe that now? That's the truth. Upon my word and honour that's the truth. I never heard your voice sound so fresh and so ... so clear and fresh, never.

Aunt Julia smiled broadly and murmured something about compliments as she released her hand from his grasp. Mr. Browne extended his open hand towards her and said to those who were near him in the manner of a showman introducing a prodigy to an audience:

—Miss Julia Morkan, my latest discovery!

He was laughing very heartily at this himself when Freddy Malins turned to him and said:

—Well, Browne, if you're serious you might make a worse discovery. All I can say is I never heard her sing half so well as long as I am coming here. And that's the honest truth.

—Neither did I, said Mr. Browne. I think her voice has greatly improved.

Aunt Julia shrugged her shoulders and said with meek pride:

—Thirty years ago I hadn't a bad voice as voices go.

—I often told Julia, said aunt Kate emphatically, that she was simply thrown away in that choir. But she never would be said by[1] me.

She turned as if to appeal to the good sense of the others against a refractory child while aunt Julia gazed in front of her, a vague smile of reminiscence playing on her face.

—No, continued aunt Kate, she wouldn't be said or led by anyone, slaving there in that choir night and day, night and day. Six o'clock on Christmas morning! And all for what?

—Well, isn't it for the honour of God, aunt Kate? asked Mary Jane twisting round on the piano stool and smiling.

Aunt Kate turned fiercely on her niece and said:

—I know all about the honour of God, Mary Jane, but I think it's not at all honourable for the pope to turn out the women out of the choirs[2] that have slaved there all their lives and put little whip-

---

1 *be said by* Be ruled by; submit to.

2 *pope ... choirs* In his 1903 *Motu Propio* on sacred music, the new pope, Pope Pius X, forbade women from singing in church choirs. Soprano and alto parts, he dictated, would henceforward be performed by boys, who, unlike women, could hold liturgical office. For more information, see appendix C.3, "Women and Catholic Church Choirs," in the "In Context" materials.

persnappers of boys over their heads. I suppose it is for the good of the church if the pope does it. But it's not just, Mary Jane, and it's not right.

She had worked herself into a passion and would have continued in defence of her sister for it was a sore subject with her but Mary Jane, seeing that all the dancers had come back, intervened pacifically:

—Now, aunt Kate, you're giving scandal to Mr. Browne who is of the other persuasion.[1]

Aunt Kate turned to Mr. Browne, who was grinning at this allusion to his religion, and said hastily:

—O, I don't question the pope's being right. I'm only a stupid old woman and I wouldn't presume to do such a thing. But there's such a thing as common everyday politeness and gratitude. And if I were in Julia's place I'd tell that Father Healy straight up to his face ...

—And besides, aunt Kate, said Mary Jane, we really are all hungry and when we are hungry we are all very quarrelsome.

—And when we are thirsty we are also quarrelsome, added Mr. Browne.

—So that we had better go to supper, said Mary Jane, and finish the discussion afterwards.

On the landing outside the drawingroom Gabriel found his wife and Mary Jane trying to persuade Miss Ivors to stay for supper. But Miss Ivors, who had put on her hat and was buttoning her cloak, would not stay. She did not feel in the least hungry and she had already overstayed her time.

—But only for ten minutes, Molly, said Mrs. Conroy. That won't delay you.

—To take a pick itself,[2] said Mary Jane, after all your dancing.

—I really couldn't, said Miss Ivors.

—I am afraid you didn't enjoy yourself at all, said Mary Jane hopelessly.

—Ever so much, I assure you, said Miss Ivors, but you really must let me run off now.

—But how can you get home? asked Mrs. Conroy.

—O, it's only two steps up the quay.

Gabriel hesitated a moment and said:

---

1 *of the other persuasion* I.e., Protestant.
2 *a pick itself* I.e., a little bit.

—If you will allow me, Miss Ivors, I'll see you home if you really are obliged to go.

But Miss Ivors broke away from them.

—I won't hear of it, she cried. For goodness' sake go in to your suppers and don't mind me. I'm quite well able to take care of myself.

—Well, you're the comical girl, Molly, said Mrs. Conroy frankly.

—*Beannacht libh*,[1] cried Miss Ivors with a laugh as she ran down the staircase.

Mary Jane gazed after her, a moody puzzled expression on her face, while Mrs. Conroy leaned over the banisters to listen for the halldoor. Gabriel asked himself was he the cause of her abrupt departure. But she did not seem to be in ill humour: she had gone away laughing. He stared blankly down the staircase.

At that moment aunt Kate came toddling out of the supper room, almost wringing her hands in despair.

—Where is Gabriel? she cried. Where on earth is Gabriel? There's everyone waiting in there, stage to let, and nobody to carve the goose!

—Here I am, aunt Kate! cried Gabriel with sudden animation, ready to carve a flock of geese, if necessary.

A fat brown goose lay at one end of the table and at the other end, on a bed of creased paper strewn with sprigs of parsley, lay a great ham, stripped of its outer skin and peppered over with crust crumbs, a neat paper frill round its shin, and beside this was a round of spiced beef. Between these rival ends ran parallel lines of side dishes: two little minsters of jelly, red and yellow, a shallow dish full of blocks of blancmange[2] and red jam, a large green leafshaped dish with a stalkshaped handle on which lay bunches of purple raisins and peeled almonds, a companion dish on which lay a solid rectangle of Smyrna figs, a dish of custard topped with grated nutmeg, a small bowl full of chocolates and sweets wrapped in gold and silver papers and a glass vase in which stood some tall celery stalks. In the centre of the table there stood, as sentries to a fruit stand which upheld a pyramid of oranges and American apples, two squat oldfashioned decanters of cut glass, one containing port and the other dark sherry. On the closed square piano a pudding in a huge yellow dish lay in waiting

---

1 *Beannacht libh* An Irish farewell; literally, "my blessings go with you."
2 *blancmange* Milk jelly.

and behind it were three squads of bottles of stout and ale and minerals drawn up according to the colours of their uniforms, the first two black with brown and red labels, the third and smallest squad white, with transverse green sashes.

Gabriel took his seat boldly at the head of the table and, having looked to the edge of the carver, plunged his fork firmly into the goose. He felt quite at ease now for he was an expert carver and liked nothing better than to find himself at the head of a well laden table.

—Miss Furlong, what shall I send you? he asked. A wing or a slice of the breast?

—Just a small slice of the breast.

—Miss Higgins, what for you?

—O, anything at all, Mr. Conroy.

While Gabriel and Miss Daly exchanged plates of goose and plates of ham and spiced beef Lily went from guest to guest with a dish of hot floury potatoes wrapped in a white napkin. This was Mary Jane's idea and she had also suggested apple sauce for the goose but aunt Kate had said that plain roast goose without any apple sauce had always been good enough for her and she hoped she might never eat worse. Mary Jane waited on her pupils and saw that they got the best slices and aunt Kate and aunt Julia opened and carried across from the piano bottles of stout and ale for the gentlemen and bottles of minerals for the ladies. There was a great deal of confusion and laughter and noise, the noise of orders and counterorders, of knives and forks, of corks and glass stoppers. Gabriel began to carve second helpings as soon as he had finished the first round without serving himself. Everyone protested loudly so that he compromised by taking a long draught of stout for he had found the carving hot work. Mary Jane settled down quietly to her supper but aunt Kate and aunt Julia were still toddling round the table, walking on each other's heels, getting in each other's way and giving each other unheeded orders. Mr. Browne begged of them to sit down and eat their supper and so did Gabriel but they said there was time enough so that, at last, Freddy Malins stood up and, capturing aunt Kate, plumped her down on her chair amid general laughter.

When everyone had been well served Gabriel said smiling:

—Now if anyone wants a little more of what vulgar people call stuffing let him or her speak.

A chorus of voices invited him to begin his own supper and Lily came forward with three potatoes which she had reserved for him.

—Very well, said Gabriel amiably as he took another preparatory draught, kindly forget my existence, ladies and gentlemen, for a few minutes.

He set to his supper and took no part in the conversation with which the table covered Lily's removal of the plates. The subject of talk was the opera company which was then at the Theatre Royal. Mr. Bartell D'Arcy, the tenor, a dark-complexioned young man with a smart moustache, praised very highly the leading contralto of the company but Miss Furlong thought she had a rather vulgar style of production. Freddy Malins said there was a negro chieftain singing in the second part of the Gaiety pantomime who had one of the finest tenor voices he had ever heard.

—Have you heard him? he asked Mr. Bartell D'Arcy across the table.

—No, answered Mr. Bartell D'Arcy carelessly.

—Because, Freddy Malins explained, now I'd be curious to hear your opinion of him. I think he has a grand voice.

—It takes Teddy to find out the really good things, said Mr. Browne familiarly to the table.

—And why couldn't he have a voice too? asked Freddy Malins sharply. Is it because he's only a black?

Nobody answered this question and Mary Jane led the table back to the legitimate opera. One of her pupils had given her a pass for *Mignon*.[1] Of course, it was very fine, she said, but it made her think of poor Georgina Burns.[2] Mr. Browne could go back farther still to the old Italian companies that used to come to Dublin, Tietjens, Trebelli, Ilma de Murzka, Campanini, the great Giuglini, Ravelli, Aramburo. Those were the days, he said, when there was something like singing to be heard in Dublin. He told too of how the top gallery of the old Royal used to be packed night after night, of how one night an Italian tenor had sung five encores to *Let Me Like a Soldier Fall*,[3] introducing

---

1   *Mignon*   1866 opera by French composer Ambroise Thomas, based on *Wilhelm Meister's Apprenticeship* (1795–96), a novel by the German writer Goethe.
2   *Georgina Burns*   Soprano who died young.
3   *Let Me ... Solider Fall*   Song from the opera *Maritana* (1845), by Irish composer William Vincent Wallace.

a high C every time, and of how the gallery boys would sometimes in their enthusiasm unyoke the horses from the carriage of some great *prima donna* and pull her themselves through the streets to her hotel. Why did they never play the grand old operas now, he asked. *Dinorah, Lucrezia Borgia?*[1] Because they could not get the voices to sing them: that was why.

—O, well, said Mr. Bartell D'Arcy, I presume there are as good singers today as there were then.

—Where are they? asked Mr. Browne defiantly.

—In London, Paris, Milan, said Mr. Bartell D'Arcy warmly. I suppose Caruso,[2] for example, is quite as good, if not better than any of the men you have mentioned.

—Maybe so, said Mr. Browne. But I may tell you I doubt it strongly.

—O, I'd give anything to hear Caruso sing, said Mary Jane.

—For me, said aunt Kate, who had been picking a bone, there was only one tenor. To please me, I mean. But I suppose none of you ever heard of him.

—Who was he, Miss Morkan? asked Mr. Bartell D'Arcy politely.

—His name, said aunt Kate, was Parkinson.[3] I heard him when he was in his prime and I think he had then the purest tenor voice that was ever put into a man's throat.

—Strange, said Mr. Bartell D'Arcy. I never even heard of him.

—Yes, yes, Miss Morkan is right, said Mr. Browne. I remember hearing of old Parkinson but he's too far back for me.

—A beautiful pure sweet mellow English tenor, said aunt Kate with enthusiasm.

Gabriel having finished, the huge pudding was transferred to the table. The clatter of forks and spoons began again. Gabriel's wife served out spoonfuls of the pudding and passed the plates down the table. Midway down they were held up by Mary Jane who replenished them with raspberry or orange jelly or with blancmange and jam. The pudding was of aunt Julia's making and she received praises

---

1 *Dinorah* 1859 opera by Giacomo Meyerbeer; *Lucrezia Borgia* 1833 opera by Gaetano Donizetti, based on Victor Hugo's 1833 play of the same name.

2 *Caruso* Tenor Enrico Caruso (1874–1921).

3 *Parkinson* The identity of this singer is unknown, and may be fictional.

for it from all quarters. She herself said that it was not quite brown enough.

—Well, I hope, Miss Morkan, said Mr. Browne, that I'm brown enough for you because, you know, I'm all brown.

All the gentlemen, except Gabriel, ate some of the pudding out of compliment to aunt Julia. As Gabriel never ate sweets the celery had been left for him. Freddy Malins also took a stalk of celery and ate it with his pudding. He had been told that celery was a capital thing for the blood and he was just then under doctor's care. Mrs. Malins, who had been silent all through the supper, said that her son was going down to Mount Melleray[1] in a week or so. The table then spoke of Mount Melleray, how bracing the air was down there, how hospitable the monks were and how they never asked for a penny-piece from their guests.

—And do you mean to say, asked Mr. Browne incredulously, that a chap can go down there and put up there as if it were a hotel and live on the fat of the land and then come away without paying a farthing?

—O, most people give some donation to the monastery when they leave, said Mary Jane.

—I wish we had an institution like that in our church, said Mr. Browne candidly.

He was astonished to hear that the monks never spoke, got up at two in the morning and slept in their coffins.[2] He asked what they did it for.

—That's the rule of the order, said aunt Kate firmly.

—Yes, but why? asked Mr. Browne.

Aunt Kate repeated that it was the rule, that was all. Mr. Browne still seemed not to understand. Freddy Malins explained to him, as best he could, that the monks were trying to make up for the sins committed by all the sinners in the outside world. The explanation was not very clear for Mr. Browne grinned and said:

—I like that idea very much but wouldn't a comfortable spring bed do them as well as a coffin?

---

1   *Mount Melleray*   Site of a Trappist monastery known as a retreat for people with drinking problems.

2   *slept in their coffins*   The monks slept in their habits and were buried in open coffins, but did not, in fact, sleep in their coffins.

—The coffin, said Mary Jane, is to remind them of their last end.
As the subject had grown lugubrious it was buried in a silence
of the table during which Mrs. Malins could be heard saying to her
neighbour in an indistinct undertone:

—They are very good men, the monks, very pious men.

The raisins and almonds and figs and apples and oranges and
chocolates and sweets were now passed about the table and aunt Julia
invited all the guests to have either port or sherry. At first Mr. Bartell
D'Arcy refused to take either but one of his neighbours nudged him
and whispered something to him upon which he allowed his glass to
be filled. Gradually as the last glasses were being filled the conversation ceased. A pause followed, broken only by the noise of the wine
and by unsettlings of chairs. The Misses Morkan, all three, looked
down at the tablecloth. Someone coughed once or twice and then
a few gentlemen patted the table gently as a signal for silence. The
silence came and Gabriel pushed back his chair and stood up.

The patting at once grew louder in encouragement and then ceased
altogether. Gabriel leaned his ten trembling fingers on the tablecloth
and smiled nervously at the company. Meeting a row of upturned faces
he raised his eyes to the chandelier. The piano was playing a waltz tune
and he could hear the skirts sweeping against the drawingroom door.
People perhaps were standing in the snow on the quay outside, gazing
up at the lighted windows and listening to the waltz music. The air was
pure there. In the distance lay the park where the trees were weighted
with snow. The Wellington monument wore a gleaming cap of snow
that flashed westward over the white field of Fifteen Acres.[1]

He began:

—Ladies and gentlemen.

— It has fallen to my lot this evening as in years past to perform a
very pleasing task, but a task for which I am afraid my poor powers as
a speaker are all too inadequate.

—No, no, said Mr. Browne.

—But, however that may be, I can only ask you tonight to take the
will for the deed and to lend me your attention for a few moments
while I endeavour to express to you in words what my feelings are on
this occasion.

---

1   *Fifteen Acres*   Large field in Phoenix Park, the Dublin park where the Wellington Monument is also located.

—Ladies and gentlemen. It is not the first time that we have gathered together under this hospitable roof, around this hospitable board. It is not the first time that we have been the recipients—or, perhaps I had better say, the victims—of the hospitality of certain good ladies.

He made a circle in the air with his arm and paused. Everyone laughed or smiled at aunt Kate and aunt Julia and Mary Jane who all turned crimson with pleasure. Gabriel went on more boldly:

—I feel more strongly with every recurring year that our country has no tradition which does it so much honour and which it should guard so jealously as that of its hospitality. It is a tradition that is unique so far as my experience goes (and I have visited not a few places abroad) among the modern nations. Some would say, perhaps, that with us it is rather a failing than anything to be boasted of. But granted even that, it is, to my mind, a princely failing and one that I trust will long be cultivated among us. Of one thing, at least, I am sure. As long as this one roof shelters the good ladies aforesaid—and I wish from my heart it may do so for many and many a long year to come—the tradition of genuine warmhearted courteous Irish hospitality, which our forefathers have handed down to us and which we in turn must hand down to our descendants, is still alive among us.

A hearty murmur of assent ran round the table. It shot through Gabriel's mind that Miss Ivors was not there and that she had gone away discourteously: and he said with confidence in himself:

—Ladies and gentlemen.

—A new generation is growing up in our midst, a generation actuated by new ideas and new principles. It is serious and enthusiastic for these new ideas and its enthusiasm, even when it is misdirected, is, I believe, in the main sincere. But we are living in a sceptical and, if I may use the phrase, a thoughttormented age: and sometimes I fear that this new generation, educated or hypereducated as it is, will lack those qualities of humanity, of hospitality, of kindly humour which belonged to an older day. Listening tonight to the names of all those great singers of the past it seemed to me, I must confess, that we were living in a less spacious age. Those days might without exaggeration be called spacious days: and if they are gone beyond recall let us hope, at least, that in gatherings such as this we shall still speak of them with pride and affection, still cherish in our hearts the memory of those dead and gone great ones whose fame the world will not willingly let die.

—Hear! hear! said Mr. Browne loudly.

—But yet, continued Gabriel, his voice falling into a softer inflection, there are always in gatherings such as this sadder thoughts that will recur to our minds: thoughts of the past, of youth, of changes, of absent faces that we miss here tonight. Our path through life is strewn with many such sad memories: and were we to brood upon them always we could not find the heart to go on bravely with our work among the living. We have all of us living duties and living affections which claim, and rightly claim, our strenuous endeavours.

—Therefore I will not linger on the past. I will not let any gloomy moralising intrude upon us here tonight. Here we are gathered together for a brief moment from the bustle and rush of our everyday routine. We are met here as friends, in the spirit of good fellowship, as colleagues also, to a certain extent, in the true spirit of *camaraderie*, and as the guests of—what shall I call them?—the three Graces of the Dublin musical world.

The table burst into applause and laughter at this sally. Aunt Julia vainly asked each of her neighbours in turn to tell her what Gabriel had said.

—He says we are the three Graces, aunt Julia, said Mary Jane.

Aunt Julia did not understand but she looked up, smiling, at Gabriel who continued in the same vein:

—Ladies and gentlemen.

—I will not attempt to play tonight the part that Paris played on another occasion. I will not attempt to choose between them. The task would be an invidious one and one beyond my poor powers. For when I view them in turn, whether it be our chief hostess herself, whose good heart, whose too good heart, has become a byword with all who know her, or her sister, who seems to be gifted with perennial youth and whose singing must have been a surprise and a revelation to us all tonight, or, last but not least, when I consider our youngest hostess, talented, cheerful, hard-working and the best of nieces, I confess, ladies and gentlemen, that I do not know to which of them I should award the prize.

Gabriel glanced down at his aunts and, seeing the large smile on aunt Julia's face and the tears which had risen to aunt Kate's eyes, hastened to his close. He raised his glass of port gallantly while every member of the company fingered a glass expectantly and said loudly:

—Let us toast them all three together. Let us drink to their health, wealth, long life, happiness and prosperity and may they long continue to hold the proud and selfwon position which they hold in their profession and the position of honour and affection which they hold in our hearts.

All the guests stood up, glass in hand and, turning towards the three seated ladies, sang in unison with Mr. Browne as leader:

—For they are jolly gay fellows,
For they are jolly gay fellows,
For they are jolly gay fellows
Which nobody can deny.

Aunt Kate was making frank use of her handkerchief and even aunt Julia seemed moved. Freddy Malins beat time with his pudding fork and the singers turned towards one another as if in melodious conference, while they sang with emphasis:

—Unless he tells a lie,
Unless he tells a lie.

Then turning once more towards their hostesses they sang:

—For they are jolly gay fellows,
For they are jolly gay fellows,
For they are jolly gay fellows
Which nobody can deny.

The acclamation which followed was taken up beyond the door of the supper room by many of the other guests and renewed time after time, Freddy Malins acting as officer with his fork on high.

*   *   *

The piercing morning air came into the hall where they were standing so that aunt Kate said:

—Close the door, somebody. Mrs. Malins will get her death of cold.

—Browne is out there, aunt Kate, said Mary Jane.

—Browne is everywhere, said aunt Kate lowering her voice.

Mary Jane laughed at her tone.

—Really, she said archly, he is very attentive.

—He has been laid on here like the gas,[1] said aunt Kate in the same tone, all during the Christmas.

She laughed herself this time good-humouredly and then added quickly:

—But tell him to come in, Mary Jane, and close the door. I hope to goodness he didn't hear me.

At that moment the halldoor was opened and Mr. Browne came in from the doorstep, laughing as if his heart would break. He was dressed in a long green overcoat with mock astrakhan[2] cuffs and collar and wore on his head an oval fur cap. He pointed down the snowcovered quay whence the sound of shrill prolonged whistling was borne in.

—Teddy will have all the cabs in Dublin out, he said.

Gabriel advanced from the little pantry behind the office, struggling into his overcoat and, looking round the hall, said:

—Gretta not down yet?

—She's getting on her things, Gabriel, said aunt Kate.

—Who's playing up there? asked Gabriel.

—Nobody. They're all gone.

—O no, aunt Kate, said Mary Jane. Bartell D'Arcy and Miss O'Callaghan aren't gone yet.

—Someone is strumming at the piano, anyhow, said Gabriel.

Mary Jane glanced at Gabriel and Mr. Browne and said with a shiver:

—It makes me feel cold to look at you two gentlemen muffled up like that. I wouldn't like to face your journey home at this hour.

—I'd like nothing better this minute, said Mr. Browne stoutly, than a rattling fine walk in the country or a fast drive with a good spanking goer between the shafts.

—We used to have a very good horse and trap[3] at home, said Aunt Julia sadly.

—The never-to-be-forgotten Johnny, said Mary Jane laughing.

Aunt Kate and Gabriel laughed too.

—Why, what was wonderful about Johnny? asked Mr. Browne.

---

1   *laid on ... the gas*   Permanently installed, like the gas supply.
2   *astrakhan*   Lambskin.
3   *trap*   Small, two-wheeled carriage on springs.

—The late lamented Patrick Morkan, our grandfather that is, explained Gabriel, commonly known in his later years as the old gentleman, was a glue boiler.

—O now, Gabriel, said aunt Kate laughing, he had a starch mill.

—Well, glue or starch, said Gabriel, the old gentleman had a horse by the name of Johnny. And Johnny used to work in the old gentleman's mill walking round and round in order to drive the mill. That was all very well; but now comes the tragic part about Johnny. One fine day the old gentleman thought he'd like to drive out with the quality to a military review in the park.

—The Lord have mercy on his soul, said aunt Kate compassionately.

—Amen, said Gabriel. So the old gentleman, as I said, harnessed Johnny and put on his very best tall hat and his very best stock collar and drove out in grand style from his ancestral mansion somewhere near Back Lane, I think.

Everyone laughed, even Mrs. Malins, at Gabriel's manner and aunt Kate said:

—O now, Gabriel, he didn't live in Back Lane really. Only the mill was there.

—Out from the mansion of his forefathers, continued Gabriel, he drove with Johnny. And everything went on beautifully until Johnny came in sight of King Billy's statue:[1] and whether he fell in love with the horse King Billy sits on or whether he thought he was back again in the mill, anyhow he began to walk round the statue.

Gabriel paced in a circle round the hall in his goloshes amid the laughter of the others.

—Round and round he went, said Gabriel, and the old gentleman, who was a very pompous old gentleman, was highly indignant. *Go on, sir! What do you mean, sir? Johnny! Johnny! Most extraordinary conduct! Can't understand the horse!*

The peals of laughter which followed Gabriel's imitation of the incident were interrupted by a resounding knock at the halldoor. Mary Jane ran to open it and let in Freddy Malins. Freddy Malins, with his

---

1 *King Billy's statue* Equestrian statue of King William III (William of Orange), a Protestant King of England who defeated the Irish Catholic forces at the Battle of the Boyne (1690).

hat well back on his head and his shoulders humped with cold, was puffing and steaming after his exertions.

—I could only get one cab, he said.

—O, we'll find another along the quay, said Gabriel.

—Yes, said aunt Kate. Better not keep Mrs. Malins standing in the draught.

Mrs. Malins was helped down the front steps by her son and Mr. Browne and, after many manoeuvres, hoisted into the cab. Freddy Malins clambered in after her and spent a long time settling her on the seat, Mr. Browne helping him with advice. At last she was settled comfortably and Freddy Malins invited Mr. Browne into the cab. There was a good deal of confused talk, then Mr. Browne got into the cab. The cabman settled his rug over his knees and bent down for the address. The confusion grew greater and the cabman was directed differently by Freddy Malins and Mr. Browne, each of whom had his head out through a window of the cab. The difficulty was to know where to drop Mr. Browne along the route and aunt Kate, aunt Julia and Mary Jane helped the discussion from the doorstep with cross-directions and contradictions and abundance of laughter. As for Freddy Malins he was speechless with laughter. He popped his head in and out of the window every moment, to the great danger of his hat, and told his mother how the discussion was progressing till at last Mr. Browne shouted to the bewildered cabman above the din of everybody's laughter:

—Do you know Trinity College?

—Yes, sir, said the cabman.

—Well, drive bang up against Trinity College gates, said Mr. Browne, and then we'll tell you where to go. You understand now?

—Yes, sir, said the cabman.

—Make like a bird for Trinity College.

—Right, sir, cried the cabman.

The horse was whipped up and the cab rattled off along the quay amid a chorus of laughter and adieus.

Gabriel had not gone to the door with the others. He was in a dark part of the hall gazing up the staircase. A woman was standing near the top of the first flight in the shadow also. He could not see her face but he could see the terracotta and salmonpink panels of her skirt which the shadow made appear black and white. It was his wife.

She was leaning on the banisters listening to something. Gabriel was surprised at her stillness and strained his ear to listen also. But he could hear little save the noise of laughter and dispute on the front steps, a few chords struck on the piano and a few notes of a man's voice singing.

He stood still in the gloom of the hall, trying to catch the air that the voice was singing and gazing up at his wife. There was grace and mystery in her attitude as if she were a symbol of something. He asked himself what is a woman standing on the stairs in the shadow, listening to distant music, a symbol of. If he were a painter he would paint her in that attitude. Her blue felt hat would show off the bronze of her hair against the darkness and the dark panels of her skirt would show off the light ones. *Distant Music* he would call the picture if he were a painter.

The halldoor was closed and aunt Kate, aunt Julia and Mary Jane came down the hall, still laughing.

—Well, isn't Freddy terrible? said Mary Jane. He's really terrible.

Gabriel said nothing but pointed up the stairs towards where his wife was standing. Now that the halldoor was closed the voice and the piano could be heard more clearly. Gabriel held up his hand for them to be silent. The song seemed to be in the old Irish tonality and the singer seemed uncertain both of his words and of his voice. The voice made plaintive by the distance and by the singer's hoarseness faintly illuminated the cadence of the air with words expressing grief:

> —O, the rain falls on my heavy locks
> And the dew wets my skin,
> My babe lies cold ... [1]

—O, exclaimed Mary Jane. It's Bartell D'Arcy singing and he wouldn't sing all the night. O, I'll get him to sing a song before he goes.

—O do, Mary Jane, said aunt Kate.

Mary Jane brushed past the others and ran to the staircase but before she reached it the singing stopped and the piano was closed abruptly.

---

1 *O, the rain ... lies cold* Lines from "The Lass of Aughrim," a popular ballad about tragic love that originated in Scotland (as "The Lass of Roch Royall") and circulated throughout Ireland.

—O, what a pity! she cried. Is he coming down, Gretta?

Gabriel heard his wife answer yes and saw her come down towards them. A few steps behind her were Mr. Bartell D'Arcy and Miss O'Callaghan.

—O, Mr. D'Arcy, cried Mary Jane, it's downright mean of you to break off like that when we were all in raptures listening to you.

—I have been at him all the evening, said Miss O'Callaghan, and Mrs. Conroy too, and he told us he had a dreadful cold and couldn't sing.

—O, Mr. D'Arcy, said aunt Kate, now that was a great fib to tell.

—Can't you see that I'm as hoarse as a crow? said Mr. D'Arcy roughly.

He went into the pantry hastily and put on his overcoat. The others, taken aback by his rude speech, could find nothing to say. Aunt Kate wrinkled her brows and made signs to the others to drop the subject. Mr. D'Arcy stood swathing his neck carefully and frowning.

—It's the weather, said aunt Julia after a pause.

—Yes, everybody has colds, said aunt Kate readily, everybody.

—They say, said Mary Jane, we haven't had snow like it for thirty years: and I read this morning in the newspaper that the snow is general all over Ireland.

—I love the look of snow, said aunt Julia sadly.

—So do I, said Miss O'Callaghan. I think Christmas is never really Christmas unless we have the snow on the ground.

—But poor Mr. D'Arcy doesn't like the snow, said aunt Kate smiling.

Mr. D'Arcy came from the pantry, fully swathed and buttoned, and in a repentant tone told them the history of his cold. Everyone gave him advice and said it was a great pity and urged him to be very careful of his throat in the night air. Gabriel watched his wife who did not join in the conversation. She was standing right under the dusty fanlight and the flame of the gas lit up the rich bronze of her hair which he had seen her drying at the fire a few days before. She was in the same attitude and seemed unaware of the talk about her. At last she turned towards them and Gabriel saw that there was colour on her cheeks and that her eyes were shining. A sudden tide of joy went leaping out of his heart.

—Mr. D'Arcy, she said, what is the name of that song you were singing?

—It's called *The Lass of Aughrim*, said Mr. D'Arcy, but I couldn't remember it properly. Why? Do you know it?

—*The Lass of Aughrim*, she repeated. I couldn't think of the name.

—It's a very nice air, said Mary Jane. I'm sorry you were not in voice tonight.

—Now, Mary Jane, said aunt Kate, don't annoy Mr. D'Arcy. I won't have him annoyed.

Seeing that all were ready to start she shepherded them to the door where goodnight was said:

—Well, goodnight aunt Kate, and thanks for the pleasant evening.

—Goodnight, Gabriel. Goodnight, Gretta!

—Goodnight, aunt Kate, and thanks ever so much. Goodnight, aunt Julia.

—O, goodnight, Gretta, I didn't see you.

—Goodnight, Mr. D'Arcy. Goodnight, Miss O'Callaghan.

—Goodnight, Miss Morkan.

—Goodnight again.

—Goodnight all. Safe home.

—Goodnight. Goodnight.

The morning was still dark. A dull yellow light brooded over the houses and the river and the sky seemed to be descending. It was slushy underfoot and only streaks and patches of snow lay on the roofs, on the parapets of the quay and on the area railings. The lamps were still burning redly in the murky air and, across the river, the palace of the Four Courts[1] stood out menacingly against the heavy sky.

She was walking on before him with Mr. Bartell D'Arcy, her shoes in a brown parcel tucked under one arm and her hands holding her skirt up from the slush. She had no longer any grace of attitude but Gabriel's eyes were still bright with happiness. The blood went bounding along his veins and the thoughts went rioting through his brain, proud, joyful, tender, valorous.

She was walking on before him so lightly and so erect that he longed to run after her noiselessly, catch her by the shoulders and say something foolish and affectionate into her ear. She seemed to

---

1 *palace of the Four Courts* Irish law courts.

him so frail that he longed to defend her against something and then to be alone with her. Moments of their secret life together burst like stars upon his memory. A heliotrope[1] envelope was lying beside his breakfast cup and he was caressing it with his hand. Birds were twittering in the ivy and the sunny web of the curtain was shimmering along the floor: he could not eat for happiness. They were standing on the crowded platform and he was placing a ticket inside the warm palm of her glove. He was standing with her in the cold, looking in through a grated window at a man making bottles in a roaring furnace. It was very cold. Her face, fragrant in the cold air, was quite close to his and suddenly she called out to the man at the furnace:

—Is the fire hot, sir?

But the man could not hear her with the noise of the furnace. It was just as well. He might have answered rudely.

A wave of yet more tender joy escaped from his heart and went coursing in warm flood along his arteries. Like the tender fire of stars moments of their life together, that no one knew of or would ever know of, broke upon and illumined his memory. He longed to recall to her those moments, to make her forget the years of their dull existence together and remember only their moments of ecstasy. For the years, he felt, had not quenched his soul or hers. Their children, his writing, her household cares had not quenched all their souls' tender fire. In one letter that he had written to her then he had said: *Why is it that words like these seem to me so dull and cold? Is it because there is no word tender enough to be your name?*

Like distant music these words that he had written years before were borne towards him from the past. He longed to be alone with her. When the others had gone away, when he and she were in their room in the hotel, then they would be alone together. He would call her softly:

—Gretta!

Perhaps she would not hear at once: she would be undressing. Then something in his voice would strike her. She would turn and look at him ....

---

1 *heliotrope* Purple, like the flowers on the heliotrope plant.

At the corner of Winetavern Street they met a cab. He was glad of its rattling noise as it saved him from conversation. She was looking out of the window and seemed tired. The others spoke only a few words, pointing out some building or street. The horse galloped along wearily under the murky morning sky, dragging his old rattling box after his heels, and Gabriel was again in a cab with her galloping to catch the boat, galloping to their honeymoon.

As the cab drove across O'Connell bridge Miss O'Callaghan said:

—They say you never cross O'Connell bridge without seeing a white horse.

—I see a white man this time, said Gabriel.

—Where? asked Mr. Bartell D'Arcy.

Gabriel pointed to the statue[1] on which lay patches of snow. Then he nodded familiarly to it and waved his hand.

—Goodnight, Dan, he said gaily.

When the cab drew up before the hotel Gabriel jumped out and, in spite of Mr. Bartell D'Arcy's protest, paid the driver. He gave the man a shilling over his fare. The man saluted and said:

—A prosperous new year to you, sir.

—The same to you, said Gabriel cordially.

She leaned for a moment on his arm in getting out of the cab and while standing at the kerbstone bidding the others goodnight. She leaned lightly on his arm, as lightly as when she had danced with him a few hours before. He had felt proud and happy then, happy that she was his, proud of her grace and wifely carriage. But now after the kindling again of so many memories, the first touch of her body, musical and strange and perfumed, sent through him a keen pang of lust. Under cover of her silence he pressed her arm closely to his side: and, as they stood at the hotel door, he felt that they had escaped from their lives and duties, escaped from home and friends and run away together with wild and radiant hearts to a new adventure.

An old man was dozing in a great hooded chair in the hall. He lit a candle in the office and went before them to the stairs. They followed him in silence, their feet falling in soft thuds on the thickly carpeted

---

1   *the statue*   The O'Connell Memorial, commemorating Irish nationalist Daniel O'Connell (1775–1847).

stairs. She mounted the stairs behind the porter, her head bowed in the ascent, her frail shoulders curved as with a burden, her skirt girt tightly about her. He could have flung his arms about her hips and held her still for his arms were trembling with desire to seize her and only the stress of his nails against the palms of his hands held the wild impulse of his body in check. The porter halted on the stairs to settle his guttering candle. They halted too on the steps below him. In the silence Gabriel could hear the falling of the molten wax into the tray and the thumping of his own heart against his ribs.

The porter led them along a corridor and opened a door. Then he set his unstable candle down on a toilet table and asked at what hour they were to be called in the morning.

—Eight, said Gabriel.

The porter pointed to the tap of the electric light and began a muttered apology but Gabriel cut him short.

—We don't want any light. We have light enough from the street. And, I say, he added pointing to the candle, you might remove that handsome article, like a good man.

The porter took up his candle again, but slowly, for he was surprised by such a novel idea. Then he mumbled goodnight and went out. Gabriel shot the lock to.

A ghostly light from the street lamp lay in a long shaft from one window to the door. Gabriel threw his overcoat and hat on a couch and crossed the room towards the window. He looked down into the street in order that his emotion might calm a little. Then he turned and leaned against a chest of drawers with his back to the light. She had taken off her hat and cloak and was standing before a large swinging mirror, unhooking her waist. Gabriel paused for a few moments, watching her, and then said:

—Gretta!

She turned away from the mirror slowly and walked along the shaft of light towards him. Her face looked so serious and weary that the words would not pass Gabriel's lips. No, it was not the moment yet.

—You look tired, he said.

—I am a little, she answered.

—You don't feel ill or weak?

—No, tired: that's all.

She went on to the window and stood there, looking out. Gabriel waited again and then, fearing that diffidence was about to conquer him, he said abruptly:

—By the way, Gretta!

—What is it?

—You know that poor fellow Malins? he said quickly.

—Yes, what about him?

—Well, poor fellow, he's a decent sort of chap after all, continued Gabriel in a false voice. He gave me back that sovereign I lent him and I didn't expect it really. It's a pity he wouldn't keep away from that Browne because he's not a bad fellow at heart.

He was trembling now with annoyance. Why did she seem so abstracted? He did not know how he could begin. Was she annoyed too about something? If she would only turn to him or come to him of her own accord! To take her as she was would be brutal. No, he must see some ardour in her eyes first. He longed to be master of her strange mood.

—When did you lend him the pound? she asked after a pause.

Gabriel strove to restrain himself from breaking out into brutal language about the sottish Malins and his pound. He longed to cry to her from his soul, to crush her body against his, to overmaster her. But he said:

—O, at Christmas, when he opened that little Christmas card shop in Henry Street.

He was in such a fever of rage and desire that he did not hear her come from the window. She stood before him for an instant looking at him strangely. Then, suddenly raising herself on tiptoe and resting her hands lightly on his shoulders, she kissed him.

—You are a very generous person, Gabriel, she said.

Gabriel, trembling with delight at her sudden kiss and at the quaintness of her phrase, put his hands on her hair and began smoothing it back, scarcely touching it with his fingers. The washing had made it fine and brilliant. His heart was brimming over with happiness. Just when he was wishing for it she had come to him of her own accord. Perhaps her thoughts had been running with his. Perhaps she had felt the impetuous desire that was in him and then the yielding mood had come upon her. Now that she had fallen to him so easily he wondered why he had been so diffident.

He stood, holding her head between his hands. Then, slipping one arm swiftly about her body and drawing her towards him, he said softly:

—Gretta dear, what are you thinking about?

She did not answer nor yield wholly to his arm. He said again softly:

—Tell me what it is, Gretta. I think I know what is the matter. Do I know?

She did not answer at once. Then she said in an outburst of tears: —O, I am thinking about that song, *The Lass of Aughrim*.

She broke loose from him and ran to the bed and, throwing her arms across the bedrail, hid her face. Gabriel stood stockstill for a moment in astonishment and then followed her. As he passed in the way of the cheval glass he caught sight of himself in full length, his broad, wellfilled shirtfront, the face whose expression always puzzled him when he saw it in a mirror and his glimmering giltrimmed eyeglasses. He halted a few paces from her and said:

—What about the song? Why does that make you cry?

She raised her head from her arms and dried her eyes with the back of her hand like a child. A kinder note than he had intended went into his voice.

—Why, Gretta? he asked.

—I am thinking about a person long ago who used to sing that song.

—And who was the person long ago? asked Gabriel smiling.

—It was a person I used to know in Galway when I was living with my grandmother, she said.

The smile passed away from Gabriel's face. A dull anger began to gather again at the back of his mind and the dull fires of his lust began to glow angrily in his veins.

—Someone you were in love with? he asked ironically.

—It was a young boy I used to know, she answered, named Michael Furey. He used to sing that song, *The Lass of Aughrim*. He was very delicate.

Gabriel was silent. He did not wish her to think that he was interested in this delicate boy.

—I can see him so plainly, she said after a moment. Such eyes as he had, big dark eyes! And such an expression in them—an expression!…

—O, then you were in love with him? said Gabriel.

—I used to go out walking with him, she said, when I was in Galway.

A thought flew across Gabriel's mind.

—Perhaps that was why you wanted to go to Galway with that Ivors girl? he said coldly.

She looked at him and asked in surprise:

—What for?

Her eyes made Gabriel feel awkward. He shrugged his shoulders and said:

—How do I know? To see him, perhaps.

She looked away from him along the shaft of light towards the window in silence.

—He is dead, she said at length. He died when he was only seventeen. Isn't it a terrible thing to die so young as that?

—What was he? asked Gabriel, still ironically.

—He was in the gasworks, she said.

Gabriel felt humiliated by the failure of his irony and by the evocation of this figure from the dead, a boy in the gasworks. The irony of his mood soured into sarcasm. While he had been full of memories of their secret life together, full of tenderness and joy and desire, she had been comparing him in her mind with another. A shameful consciousness of his own person assailed him. He saw himself as a ludicrous figure, acting as a pennyboy for his aunts, a nervous wellmeaning sentimentalist, orating to vulgarians and idealising his own clownish lusts, the pitiable fatuous fellow he had caught a glimpse of in the mirror. Instinctively he turned his back more to the light lest she might see the shame that burned upon his forehead.

He tried to keep up his tone of cold interrogation but his voice when he spoke was humble and indifferent.

—I suppose you were in love with this Michael Furey, Gretta, he said.

—I was great with[1] him at that time, she said.

Her voice was veiled and sad. Gabriel, feeling now how vain it would be to try to lead her whither he had purposed, caressed one of her hands and said also sadly:

---

1   *great with* Friendly with.

—And what did he die of so young, Gretta? Consumption, was it?

—I think he died for me, she answered.

A vague terror seized Gabriel at this answer as if, at that hour when he had hoped to triumph, some impalpable and vindictive being was coming against him, gathering forces against him in its vague world. But he shook himself free of it with an effort of reason and continued to caress her hand. He did not question her again for he felt that she would tell him of herself. Her hand was warm and moist: it did not respond to his touch but he continued to caress it just as he had caressed her first letter to him that spring morning.

—It was in the winter, she said, about the beginning of the winter when I was going to leave my grandmother's and come up here to the convent. And he was ill at the time in his lodgings in Galway and wouldn't be let out and his people in Oughterard were written to. He was in decline, they said, or something like that. I never knew rightly.

She paused for a moment and sighed.

—Poor fellow, she said, he was very fond of me and he was such a gentle boy. We used to go out together walking, you know, Gabriel, like the way they do in the country. He was going to study singing only for his health. He had a very good voice, poor Michael Furey.

—Well, and then? asked Gabriel.

—And then when it came to the time for me to leave Galway and come up to the convent he was much worse and I wouldn't be let see him so I wrote him a letter saying I was going up to Dublin and would be back in the summer and hoping he would be better then.

She paused for a moment to get her voice under control and then went on:

—Then the night before I left I was in my grandmother's house in Nun's Island, packing up, and I heard gravel thrown up against the window. The window was so wet I couldn't see so I ran downstairs as I was and slipped out the back into the garden and there was the poor fellow at the end of the garden shivering.

—And did you not tell him to go back? asked Gabriel.

—I implored of him to go home at once and told him he would get his death in the rain. But he said he did not want to live. I can see his eyes as well as well![1] He was standing at the end of the wall where there was a tree.

---

1 *as well as well* I.e., as well as well can be.

—And did he go home? asked Gabriel.

—Yes, he went home. And when I was only a week in the convent he died and he was buried in Oughterard where his people came from. O, the day I heard that, that he was dead!....

She stopped, choking with sobs and, overcome by emotion, flung herself face downward on the bed, sobbing in the quilt. Gabriel held her hand for a moment longer, irresolutely, and then, shy of intruding on her grief, let it fall gently and walked quietly to the window.

She was fast asleep.

Gabriel, leaning on his elbow, looked for a few moments unresentfully at her tangled hair and half open mouth, listening to her deep drawn breath. So she had had that romance in her life: a man had died for her sake. It hardly pained him now to think how poor a part he, her husband, had played in her life. He watched her while she slept as though he and she had never lived together as man and wife. His curious eyes rested long upon her face and on her hair: and as he thought of what she must have been then, in that time of her first girlish beauty, a strange friendly pity for her entered his soul. He did not like to say even to himself that her face was no longer beautiful but he knew that it was no longer the face for which Michael Furey had braved death.

Perhaps she had not told him all the story. His eyes moved to the chair over which she had thrown some of her clothes. A petticoat string dangled to the floor. One boot stood upright, its limp upper fallen down: the fellow of it lay upon its side. He wondered at his riot of emotions of an hour before. From what had it proceeded? From his aunts' supper, from his own foolish speech, from the wine and dancing, the merrymaking when saying goodnight in the hall, the pleasure of the walk along the river in the snow. Poor aunt Julia! She too would soon be a shade with the shade of Patrick Morkan and his horse. He had caught that haggard look upon her face for a moment when she was singing *Arrayed for the Bridal*. Soon perhaps he would be sitting in that same drawingroom, dressed in black, his silk hat on his knees. The blinds would be drawn down and aunt Kate would be sitting beside him, crying and blowing her nose and telling him how Julia had died. He would cast about in his mind for some words that might console her and would find only lame and useless ones. Yes, yes: that would happen very soon.

The air of the room chilled his shoulders. He stretched himself cautiously along under the sheets and lay down beside his wife. One by one they were all becoming shades. Better pass boldly into that other world, in the full glory of some passion, than fade and wither dismally with age. He thought of how she who lay beside him had locked in her heart for so many years that image of her lover's eyes when he had told her that he did not wish to live.

Generous tears filled Gabriel's eyes. He had never felt like that himself towards any woman but he knew that such a feeling must be love. The tears gathered more thickly in his eyes and in the partial darkness he imagined he saw the form of a young man standing under a dripping tree. Other forms were near. His soul had approached that region where dwell the vast hosts of the dead. He was conscious of, but could not apprehend, their wayward and flickering existence. His own identity was fading out into a grey impalpable world: the solid world itself which these dead had one time reared and lived in was dissolving and dwindling.

A few light taps upon the pane made him turn to the window. It had begun to snow again. He watched sleepily the flakes, silver and dark, falling obliquely against the lamplight. The time had come for him to set out on his journey westward. Yes, the newspapers were right: snow was general all over Ireland. It was falling on every part of the dark central plain, on the treeless hills, falling softly upon the Bog of Allen and, farther westward, softly falling into the dark mutinous Shannon waves. It was falling, too, upon every part of the lonely churchyard on the hill where Michael Furey lay buried. It lay thickly drifted on the crooked crosses and headstones, on the spears of the little gate, on the barren thorns. His soul swooned slowly as he heard the snow falling faintly through the universe and faintly falling, like the descent of their last end, upon all the living and the dead.

The Gresham Hotel, c. 1900. Gabriel and Gretta retire to the Gresham Hotel after the party in "The Dead"; the cab they take would look much like the one pictured in the photograph. The "street lamp" that illuminates the room with a "ghostly light" can be seen to the left of the entrance.

In Context

A. Joyce's Other Writings

1. from James Joyce, "James Clarence Mangan" (1902)

In this laudatory essay, one of several he wrote on the Irish romantic poet James Clarence Mangan (1803–49), Joyce notes his predecessor's deft use of the concepts of chivalry, romance, and the East. Joyce employed these tropes in "Araby," in which the young protagonist's object of affection is identified simply as "Mangan's sister." For further discussion of James Clarence Mangan, see appendix D.1.

... The lore of many lands goes with him always, eastern tales and the memory of curiously printed medieval books which have rapt him out of his time—gathered together day by day and embroidered as in a web. He has acquaintance with a score of languages, of which, upon occasion, he makes a liberal parade, and has read recklessly in many literatures, crossing how many seas, and even penetrating into Peristan,[1] to which no road leads that the feet travel. In Timbuctooese, he confesses with a charming modesty which should prevent detractors, he is slightly deficient, but this is no cause for regret....

Though even in the best of Mangan the presence of alien emotions is sometimes felt the presence of an imaginative personality reflecting the light of imaginative beauty is more vividly felt. East and West meet in that personality (we know how); images interweave there like soft, luminous scarves and words ring like brilliant mail, and whether the song is of Ireland or of Istambol it has the same refrain, a prayer that peace may come again to her who has lost her peace, the moonwhite pearl of his soul, Ameen.[2] Music and odours

---

1 *Peristan* Region of Asia that includes parts of north-eastern Afghanistan, northern India, northern Pakistan, and south-western China. It has also been called Paropamisos and the Hindu Kush.
2 *Ameen* The beloved of Al-Hassan in Mangan's poem "The Last Words of Al-Hassan."

and lights are spread about her, and he would search the dews and the sands that he might set another glory near her face. A scenery and a world have grown up about her face, as they will about any face which the eyes have regarded with love. Vittoria Colonna and Laura and Beatrice[1]—even she upon whose face many lives have cast that shadowy delicacy, as of one who broods upon distant terrors and riotous dreams, and that strange stillness before which love is silent, Mona Lisa—embody one chivalrous idea, which is no mortal thing, bearing it bravely above the accidents of lust and faithlessness and weariness; and she whose white and holy hands have the virtue of enchanted hands, his virgin flower, and flower of flowers, is no less than these an embodiment of that idea. How the East is laid under tribute for her and must bring all its treasures to her feet! The sea that foams over saffron sands, the lonely cedar on the Balkans, the hall damascened with moons of gold and a breath of roses from the gulistan[2]—all these shall be where she is in willing service: reverence and peace shall be the service of the heart....

2. from James Joyce, "Ireland, Island of Saints and Sages"[3] (1907)

In this 1907 lecture, written in Italian and delivered in Trieste, then part of Austro-Hungary, Joyce surveys the variegated history of Ireland and its culture. In particular, he discusses Irish political and cultural figures and Ireland's relationship to its "two masters," England and the Catholic Church.

... It will seem strange that an island as remote as Ireland from the centre of culture could excel as a school for apostles, but even a superficial consideration will show us that the Irish nation's insistence on developing its own culture by itself is not so much the demand of a young nation that wants to make good in the European concert as

---

1   *Vittoria Colonna and Laura and Beatrice*   The muses of Michelangelo, Petrarch, and Dante, respectively.

2   *damascened*   Decorated with etched, inlaid, or beaten metal;   *gulistan*   Present-day Iran, Pakistan, Afghanistan, Azerbaijan, and Armenia all have places that bear this name.

3   *Ireland, Island of Saints and Sages*   Translation from the original Italian by Ellsworth Mason and Richard Ellmann, from *The Critical Writings of James Joyce*, Ellsworth Mason and Richard Ellmann, editors. Copyright © 1959 by Harriet Weaver and F. Lionel Monro, as administrators c.t.a. of the estate of James Joyce. Copyright renewed © 1987 by F. Lionel Monro.

the demand of a very old nation to renew under new forms the glories of a past civilisation....

Anyone who reads the history of the three centuries that precede the coming of the English[1] must have a strong stomach, because the internecine strife, and the conflicts with the Danes and the Norwegians, the black foreigners and the white foreigners, as they were called, follow each other so continuously and ferociously that they make this entire era a veritable slaughterhouse....

From the time of the English invasion to our time, there is an interval of almost eight centuries [of] foreign occupation.... [A]t that time Ireland ceased to be an intellectual force in Europe. The decorative arts, at which the ancient Irish excelled, were abandoned, and the sacred and profane culture fell into disuse....

But ... a new Celtic race was arising, compounded of the old Celtic stock and the Scandinavian, Anglo-Saxon, and Norman races. Another national temperament rose on the foundation of the old one, with the various elements mingling and renewing the ancient body. The ancient enemies made common cause against the English aggression, with the Protestant inhabitants (who had become *Hibernis Hiberniores*, more Irish than the Irish themselves) urging on the Irish Catholics in their opposition to the Calvinist and Lutheran fanatics from across the sea, and the descendants of the Danish and Norman and Anglo-Saxon settlers championing the cause of the new Irish nation against the British tyranny....

Ireland prides itself on being faithful body and soul to its national tradition as well as to the Holy See.[2] The majority of the Irish consider fidelity to these two traditions their cardinal article of faith. But the fact is that the English came to Ireland at the repeated requests of a native king, without, needless to say, any great desire on their part, and without the consent of their own king, but armed with the papal bull of Adrian IV and a papal letter of Alexander.[3] They landed on the east coast with seven hundred men, a band of adventurers

---

1   *the coming of the English*   The Norman invasion of Ireland began in 1169 CE.

2   *Holy See*   Government of the Catholic Church.

3   *Adrian IV*   Pope who, in 1155, issued a papal bull encouraging the King of England, Henry II, to invade Ireland and enforce its obedience to the Catholic Church;   *Alexander*   Adrian IV's successor, Pope Alexander III. In 1172, he issued three letters signaling his approval of Henry II's authority over Ireland.

against a nation; they were received by some native tribes, and in less than a year, the English King Henry II celebrated Christmas with gusto in the city of Dublin. In addition, there is the fact that parliamentary union was not legislated at Westminster but at Dublin, by a parliament elected by the vote of the people of Ireland, a parliament corrupted and undermined with the greatest ingenuity by the agents of the English prime minister, but an Irish parliament nevertheless.[1] From my point of view, these two facts must be thoroughly explained before the country in which they occurred has the most rudimentary right to persuade one of her sons to change his position from that of an unprejudiced observer to that of a convinced nationalist....

Our civilisation is a vast fabric, in which the most diverse elements are mingled, in which nordic aggressiveness and Roman law, the new bourgeois conventions and the remnant of a Syriac religion[2] are reconciled. In such a fabric, it is useless to look for a thread that may have remained pure and virgin without having undergone the influence of a neighbouring thread. What race, or what language (if we except the few whom a playful will seems to have preserved in ice, like the people of Iceland) can boast of being pure today? And no race has less right to utter such a boast than the race now living in Ireland. Nationality (if it really is not a convenient fiction like so many others to which the scalpels of present-day scientists have given the *coup de grâce*) must find its reason for being rooted in something that surpasses and transcends and informs changing things like blood and the human word.... Do we not see that in Ireland the Danes, the Firbolgs, the Milesians[3] from Spain, the Norman invaders, and the Anglo-Saxon settlers have united to form a new entity,

---

1 *parliamentary union ... parliament nevertheless* Although it was ruled by the same monarch as England and was politically dominated by English interests, Ireland had its own parliament from the mid-sixteenth century until the end of the eighteenth century. The "parliamentary union" Joyce refers to is the Act of Union (1800), which dissolved the Irish parliament and joined the kingdoms of Ireland and Britain to form the United Kingdom of Great Britain and Ireland.

2 *Syriac religion* I.e., Christianity.

3 *Firbolgs* Irish mythological race; in the medieval Irish pseudo-history *Lebor Gabála*, they appear as part of a series of invaders; *Milesians* The last invaders of Ireland to be described in the *Lebor Gabála*; they are sometimes considered a mythologized version of a historical Gaelic people.

one might say under the influence of a local deity? And, although the present race in Ireland is backward and inferior, it is worth taking into account the fact that it is the only race of the entire Celtic family that has not been willing to sell its birthright for a mess of pottage....

Now, what has Ireland gained by its fidelity to the papacy and its infidelity to the British crown? It has gained a great deal, but not for itself. Among the Irish writers who adopted the English language in the seventeenth and eighteenth centuries, and almost forgot their native land, are found the names of Berkeley, the idealist philosopher, Oliver Goldsmith, author of *The Vicar of Wakefield*, two famous playwrights, Richard Brinsley Sheridan and William Congreve, whose comic masterpieces are admired even today on the sterile stages of modern England, Jonathan Swift, author of *Gulliver's Travels*, which shares with Rabelais[1] the place of the best satire in world literature, and Edmund Burke, whom the English themselves called the modern Demosthenes[2] and considered the most profound orator who had ever spoken in the House of Commons.

Even today, despite her heavy obstacles, Ireland is making her contribution to English art and thought. That the Irish are really the unbalanced, helpless idiots about whom we read in the lead articles of the *Standard* and the *Morning Post* is denied by the names of the three greatest translators in English literature—FitzGerald, translator of the *Rubaiyat* of the Persian poet Omar Khayyam, Burton, translator of the Arabian masterpieces, and Cary, the classic translator of the *Divine Comedy*.[3] It is also denied by the names of other Irishmen—Arthur Sullivan, the dean of modern English music, Edward O'Connor, founder of Chartism,[4] the novelist George Moore, an intellectual oasis in the Sahara of the false spiritualistic, Messianic, and

---

1 *Rabelais* François Rabelais (1494–1553), French satirist.

2 *Demosthenes* Ancient Greek orator.

3 *FitzGerald* Poet and Translator Edward FitzGerald, best known for his translations (1859–89) of the *Rubaiyat of Omar Khayyam*, a classic collection of short verses from the early twelfth century; *Burton* Richard Francis Burton, an explorer and language scholar best known for his translation (1885–88) of the *Arabian Nights*; *Cary* Henry Francis Cary, best known for his 1814 translation of Dante's *Divine Comedy*. None of the translators mentioned were born in Ireland, but all had at least some Irish ancestry.

4 *Chartism* Working-class movement in Britain in the 1830s and 40s that argued for working-class rights, including the vote.

detective writings whose name is legion in England, by the names of two Dubliners, the paradoxical and iconoclastic writer of comedy, George Bernard Shaw, and the too well known Oscar Wilde,[1] son of a revolutionary poetess.

Finally, in the field of practical affairs this pejorative conception of Ireland is given the lie by the fact that when the Irishman is found outside of Ireland in another environment, he very often becomes a respected man. The economic and intellectual conditions that prevail in his own country do not permit the development of individuality. The soul of the country is weakened by centuries of useless struggle and broken treaties, and individual initiative is paralysed by the influence and admonitions of the church, while its body is manacled by the police, the tax office, and the garrison. No one who has any self-respect stays in Ireland, but flees afar as though from a country that has undergone the visitation of an angered Jove.

From the time of the Treaty of Limerick,[2] or rather, from the time that it was broken by the English in bad faith, millions of Irishmen have left their native land. These fugitives, as they were centuries ago, are called the wild geese. They enlisted in all the foreign brigades of the powers of Europe—France, Holland, and Spain, to be exact—and won on many battlefields the laurel of victory for their adopted masters. In America, they found another native land. In the ranks of the American rebels was heard the old Irish language, and Lord Mountjoy[3] himself said in 1784, "We have lost America through the Irish emigrants." Today, these Irish emigrants in the United States number sixteen million, a rich, powerful, and industrious settlement. Maybe this does not prove that the Irish dream of a revival is not entirely an illusion! …

Because, even today, the flight of the wild geese continues. Every year, Ireland, decimated as she already is, loses 60,000 of her sons.

---

1   *Oscar Wilde*   Playwright, poet, novelist, and celebrity (1854–1900). Joyce's descriptor "too well known" refers to the public scandal that ended in Wilde's imprisonment for "gross indecency," a vague legal term intended to punish male homosexuality.

2   *Treaty of Limerick*   Signed in 1691, this treaty ended the Williamite War (between King James II and William of Orange) and contained articles protecting the defeated Jacobite army, which was mostly composed of Irish Catholics. In 1695, a series of harsh penal laws were enacted by the Irish Parliament against Irish Catholic gentry who had not sworn loyalty to the new regime.

3   *Lord Mountjoy*   Luke Gardiner, 1st Viscount Mountjoy, an Irish politician.

From 1850 to the present day, more than 5,000,000 emigrants have left for America, and every post brings to Ireland their inviting letters to friends and relatives at home. The old men, the corrupt, the children, and the poor stay at home, where the double yoke wears another groove in the tamed neck; and around the death bed where the poor, anaemic, almost lifeless, body lies in agony, the rulers give orders and the priests administer last rites.

Is this country destined to resume its ancient position as the Hellas[1] of the north some day? Is the Celtic mind, like the Slavic mind which it resembles in many ways, destined to enrich the civil conscience with new discoveries and new insights in the future? Or must the Celtic world, the five Celtic nations, driven by stronger nations to the edge of the continent, to the outermost islands of Europe, finally be cast into the ocean after a struggle of centuries? Alas, we dilettante sociologists are only second-class augurers. We look and peer into the innards of the human animal, and, after all, confess that we see nothing there. Only our supermen know how to write the history of the future....

One thing alone seems clear to me. It is well past time for Ireland to have done once and for all with failure. If she is truly capable of reviving, let her awake, or let her cover up her head and lie down decently in her grave forever. "We Irishmen," said Oscar Wilde one day to a friend of mine,[2] "have done nothing, but we are the greatest talkers since the time of the Greeks." But though the Irish are eloquent, a revolution is not made of human breath and compromises. Ireland has already had enough equivocations and misunderstandings. If she wants to put on the play that we have waited for so long, this time let it be whole, and complete, and definitive. But our advice to the Irish producers is the same as that our fathers gave them not so long ago—hurry up! I am sure that I, at least, will never see that curtain go up, because I will have already gone home on the last train.

---

1 *Hellas* Greece.
2 *a friend of mine* Irish poet W.B. Yeats (1865–1939).

3. from James Joyce, "Gas from a Burner" (1912)

Joyce wrote this satirical poem in the voice of George Roberts, the manger of Maunsel and Company, the Dublin publishing house that refused to publish *Dubliners* after initially agreeing to do so. The publisher's reasons are summarized in the introduction to this volume.

Ladies and gents, you are here assembled
To hear why earth and heaven trembled
Because of the black and sinister arts
Of an Irish writer in foreign parts.
He sent me a book ten years ago.
I read it a hundred times or so,
Backwards and forwards, down and up,
Through both ends of a telescope.
I printed it all to the very last word
But by the mercy of the Lord
The darkness of my mind was rent
And I saw the writer's foul intent.
But I owe a duty to Ireland:
I hold her honour in my hand,
This lovely land that always sent
Her writers and artists to banishment
And in a spirit of Irish fun
Betrayed her own leaders, one by one[1]....
... I draw the line at that bloody fellow,
That was over here dressed in Austrian[2] yellow, ...
And writing of Dublin, dirty and dear,
In a manner no blackamoor printer could bear.
Shite and onions! Do you think I'll print
The name of the Wellington Monument,
Sydney Parade and Sandymount tram,

---

1   *Betrayed her ... by one*   As Joyce saw it, the Irish, acting hypocritically and foolishly, had more than once turned on their leaders, most famously in the case of Charles Stewart Parnell, Member of Parliament and founder of the Irish Parliamentary Party. After his affair with the married Katharine O'Shea became public in 1890, Parnell was abandoned by many of his former supporters, causing the collapse of the Irish Home Rule movement.

2   *Austrian*   At this time Joyce was living in Trieste, then part of Austro-Hungary.

Downes's cakeshop and Williams's jam?[1]
I'm damned if I do—I'm damned to blazes!
Talk about *Irish Names of Places*!... [2]
Who was it said: Resist not evil?
I'll burn that book,[3] so help me devil.
I'll sing a psalm as I watch it burn
And the ashes I'll keep in a one-handled urn.
I'll penance do with farts and groans
Kneeling upon my marrowbones.
This very next lent I will unbare
My penitent buttocks to the air
And sobbing besides my printing press
My awful sin I will confess.
My Irish foreman from Bannockburn
Shall dip his right hand in the urn
And sign crisscross with reverent thumb
Memento homo[4] upon my bum.

---

1   *Do you think ... Williams's jam*   Maunsel's printer feared a lawsuit based, in part, on *Dubliners'* use of actual place-names.
2   *Irish Names of Places*   Refers to *The Origin and History of Irish Names of Places* by P.W. Joyce
(no relation), popular in the latter part of the nineteenth century.
3   *Resist not ... that book*   "Resist not evil!" (Matthew 5:39) are the words of Christ. Thus, the
Bible is "that book."
4   *Memento homo*   From *Genesis* 3:19: "*Memento, homo, quia pulvis es, et in pulverem rever-
teris*" ("Remember, man, you are dust and to dust you will return"). In the Catholic Church,
the priest speaks these words on Ash Wednesday as he makes the sign of the cross on the
foreheads of the communicants.

B. Letters

1. From George Russell

This letter inadvertently gave rise to *Dubliners*. In response to Russell's request, Joyce wrote "The Sisters," followed by "Eveline" and "After the Race," all of which were published in *The Irish Homestead*. To these three, Joyce added another twelve, which collectively formed the 1914 publication *Dubliners*. See the introduction to this volume for more details.

> ? June or July 1904
> *The Irish Homestead*, Dublin,
> Editorial Department

Dear Joyce
Look at the story in this paper *The Irish Homestead*.[1] Could you write anything simple, rural?, livemaking?, pathos?, which could be inserted so as not to shock the readers. If you could furnish a short story about 1800 words suitable for insertion the editor will pay £1. It is easily earned money if you can write fluently and don't mind playing to the common understanding and liking for once in a way. You can sign it any name you like as a pseudonym.[2] Yours sincerely

> Geo. W. Russell

2. To Nora Barnacle

The last lines of Joyce's letter to Nora, written just three months after they met, echo those from a letter that Gabriel remembers having written to Gretta in "The Dead": *"Why is it that words like these seem to me so dull and cold? Is it because there is no word tender enough to be your name?"*

---

1 *the story ... Irish Homestead* See Appendix D.3 for the story Russell sent.
2 *You can ... pseudonym* Joyce signed the story "Stephen Daedalus," also the name of the protagonist of the novel-in-progress that would eventually become *A Portrait of the Artist as a Young Man* (in which Stephen's surname is spelled "Dedalus").

[26 September 1904]

7 S. Peter's Terrace, Cabra, Dublin

My dearest Nora

… How little words are necessary between us! We seem to know each other though we say nothing almost for hours…. The mere recollection of you overpowers me with some kind of dull slumber. The energy which is required for carrying on conversations seems to have left me lately and I find myself constantly slipping into silence. In a way it seems to me a pity that we do not say more to each other and yet I know how futile it is for me to remonstrate either with you or with myself for I know that when I meet you next our lips will become mute. You see how I begin to babble in these letters. And yet why should I be ashamed of words? Why should I not call you what in my heart I continually call you? What is it that prevents me unless it be that no word is tender enough to be your name?

Jim …

3. To Stanislaus Joyce

In the following letters to Stanislaus, his brother and close confidant, Joyce comments on Dublin and Irish politics.

[c. 24 September 1905]

Via S. Nicolò 30, II°, Trieste, Austria

Dear Stannie

… When you remember that Dublin has been a capital for thousands of years, that it is the "second" city of the British Empire, that it is nearly three times as big as Venice it seems strange that no artist has given it to the world….

Jim …

25 September 1906

Via Frattina 52, II, Rome

Dear Stannie,

… Sometimes thinking of Ireland it seems to me that I have been unnecessarily harsh. I have reproduced (in *Dubliners* at least) none of the attraction of the city for I have never felt at my ease in any city since I left it except in Paris. I have not reproduced its ingenuous insularity and its hospitality. The latter "virtue" so far as I can see does not exist elsewhere in Europe. I have not been just to its beauty: for it is more beautiful naturally in my opinion than what I have seen of England, Switzerland, France, Austria or Italy. And yet I know how useless these reflections are. For were I to rewrite the book as G.R.[1] suggests "in another sense" (where the hell does he get the meaningless phrases he uses) I am sure I should find again what you call the Holy Ghost sitting in the ink-bottle and the perverse devil of my literary conscience sitting on the hump of my pen....

Jim

6 November 1906
Via Frattina 52, II°, Rome

Dear Stannie,

... You ask me what I would substitute for parliamentary agitation in Ireland. I think the *Sinn Féin*[2] policy would be more effective. Of course I see that its success would be to substitute Irish for English capital but no-one, I suppose, denies that capitalism is a stage of progress. The Irish proletariat has yet to be created. A feudal peasantry exists, scraping the soil but this would with a national revival or with a definite preponderance of England surely disappear. I quite agree with you that Griffith[3] is afraid of the priests—and he has every reason to be so. But, possibly, they are also a little afraid of him too. After all, he is holding out some secular liberty to the people and the Church doesn't approve of that. I quite see, of course, that the Church is still, as it was in the time of Adrian IV,[4] the enemy of Ireland: but, I think, her time is almost up. For either *Sinn Féin* or Imperialism will conquer the present Ireland. If the Irish programme did not insist on the Irish language I suppose I could call myself a nationalist. As it is, I am content to recognise myself an exile: and, prophetically, a repudiated one....

Jim ...

---

1 *G.R.* I.e., Grant Richards.
2 *Sinn Féin* Irish: We Ourselves. *Sinn Féin* originated as an Irish nationalist party that sought to achieve Irish independence by stimulating native Irish institutions.
3 *Griffith* Arthur Griffith, founder of *Sinn Féin*.
4 *Adrian IV* Pope who, in 1155, issued a papal bull urging the English King Henry II to invade Ireland and institute Roman Catholic reforms.

4. To Grant Richards

The following letters reflect Joyce's extended conflict with the English editor Grant Richards over the publication of *Dubliners*. See the introduction to this volume for a discussion of their relationship.

5 May 1906

Via Giovanni Boccaccio 1, II, Trieste, Austria

Dear Mr. Grant Richards,

… My intention was to write a chapter of the moral history of my country and I chose Dublin for the scene because that city seemed to me the centre of paralysis. I have tried to present it to the indifferent public under four of its aspects: childhood, adolescence, maturity and public life. The stories are arranged in this order. I have written it for the most part in a style of scrupulous meanness and with the conviction that he is a very bold man who dares to alter in the presentment, still more to deform, whatever he has seen and heard. I cannot do any more than this. I cannot alter what I have written. All these objections of which the printer is now the mouthpiece arose in my mind when I was writing the book, both as to the themes of the stories and their manner of treatment. Had I listened to them I would not have written the book. I have come to the conclusion that I cannot write without offending people….

Believe me, dear Mr. Grant Richards, Faithfully yours

Jas A Joyce

20 May 1906

Via Giovanni Boccaccio 1, Trieste

Dear Mr. Grant Richards:

You say that the difficulties between us have narrowed themselves down. If this be true it is I who have narrowed them. If you will recall your first letter you will see that on your side they have broadened a little….

I mention these facts in order that you may see I have tried to meet your objections….

I have shown you that I can concede something to your fears. But you cannot really expect me to mutilate my work!...

You cannot see anything impossible and unreasonable in my position. I have explained and argued everything at full length and, when argument and explanation were unavailing, I have perforce granted what you asked, and even what you didn't ask, me to grant. The points on which I have not yielded are the points which rivet the book together. If I eliminate them what becomes of the chapter of the moral history of my country? I fight to retain them because I believe that in composing my chapter of moral history in exactly the way I have composed it I have taken the first step towards the spiritual liberation of my country. Reflect for a moment on the history of the literature of Ireland as it stands at present written in the English language before you condemn this genial illusion of mine which, after all, has at least served me in the office of a candlestick during the writing of the book. Believe me, dear Mr. Grant Richards, Faithfully yours,

Jas A Joyce

23 June 1906
Via Giovanni Boccaccio 1, Trieste

Dear Mr. Grant Richards:

... Your suggestion that those concerned in the publishing of *Dubliners* may be prosecuted for indecency is in my opinion an extraordinary contribution to the discussion. I know that some amazing imbecilities have been perpetrated in England but I really cannot see how any civilised tribunal could listen for two minutes to such an accusation against my book. I care little or nothing whether what I write is indecent or not but, if I understand the meaning of words, I have written nothing whatever indecent in *Dubliners*.

... It is not my fault that the odour of ashpits and old weeds and offal hangs round my stories. I seriously believe that you will retard the course of civilisation in Ireland by preventing the Irish people from having one good look at themselves in my nicely polished looking-glass.

Believe me, dear Mr. Grant Richards, Faithfully yours,

Jas A Joyce

C. Historical Contexts

1. from The Objects of *Inghinidhe na hÉireann*, *United Irishman* (13 October 1900)

A nationalist organization for women, *Inghinidhe na hÉireann* (Daughters of Erin) was founded in 1900. Within a few years it had merged with a number of other nationalist groups to form *Sinn Féin*, which sought to achieve Ireland's independence from England by stimulating native Irish institutions. This is the kind of organization to which Molly Ivors in "The Dead" might have belonged.

... The objects of the society are:

I. To encourage the study of Gaelic, of Irish literature, history, music, and art, especially amongst the young, by the organising and teaching of classes for the above subjects.

II. To support and popularise Irish manufactures.

III. To discourage the reading and circulation of low English literature, the singing of English songs, the attending of vulgar English entertainments at theatres and music halls, and to combat in every way English influence, which is doing so much injury to the artistic taste and refinement of the Irish people.

IV. To form a fund called the National Purposes Fund for the furtherance of the above objects....

2. from Mary Butler, "Some Suggestions as to How Irishwomen May Help the Irish Language Movement," *Gaelic League Pamphlet* No. 6 (1901)

Formed in 1893 to promote the Irish language, the Gaelic League (which uniquely admitted men and women on equal terms) managed to get Irish added to the curriculum of thousands of national schools. It played a key role in the Irish cultural revival, which Molly Ivors in "The Dead" clearly supported.

1. Realise what it means to be an Irishwoman and make others realize what it means by being Irish in fact as well as in name.

2. Make the home atmosphere Irish.
3. Make the social atmosphere Irish.
4. Speak Irish if you know it, especially in the home circle, and if you have no knowledge of the language, set about acquiring it at once. If you only know a little speak that little.
5. Insist on children learning to speak, read and write Irish.
6. Insist on school authorities giving pupils the benefit of a thoroughly Irish education.
7. Use Irish at the family prayers.
8. Give Irish names to children.
9. Visit Irish-speaking districts....
10. Encourage Irish music and song.
11. Support Irish publications and literature.
12. Employ Irish-speaking servants whenever possible.
13. Join the Gaelic League, and induce others to do so.
14. Spread the light among your acquaintances.
15. Consistently support everything Irish and consistently withhold your support from everything un-Irish.

3. Women and Catholic Church Choirs

a. from "The Singers," *Tra le Sollecitudini, Motu Proprio* (22 November 1903)

> In his 1903 *Motu Proprio* on sacred music, the new pope, Pope Pius X, forbade women from singing in church choirs. Issued just over a month before the Morkans' party (in "The Dead"), this declaration is perceived as a lack of "politeness and gratitude" by Aunt Kate. Defending the years of service her sister has put into the choir, she asserts, "it's not at all honourable for the pope to turn out the women."

... [S]ingers in church have a real liturgical office, and ... therefore women, being incapable of exercising such office, cannot be admitted to form part of the choir. Whenever, then, it is desired to employ the acute voices of sopranos and contraltos, these parts must be taken by boys, according to the most ancient usage of the Church....

Pius X, Pope

b. from Papal Letter to the Cardinal Vicar of Rome (8 December 1903)

The Pope explains his logic in a letter to Cardinal Respighi, who was to carry out his new regulation.

Lord Cardinal,

A desire to see the decorum, dignity and holiness of the liturgical functions flourishing again in all places has determined Us to make known by a special writing under Our own hand Our will with regard to the sacred music which is employed in the service of public worship. We cherish the hope that all will second Us in this desired restoration, not merely with that blind submission, always laudable though it be, which is accorded out of a pure spirit of obedience to commands that are onerous and contrary to one's own manner of thinking and feeling, but with that alacrity of will which springs from the intimate persuasion of having to do so on grounds duly weighed, clear, evident, and beyond question....

Pius X, Pope

4. from "Women Students," *Final Report of the Commissioners of the Royal Commission on Trinity College, Dublin, and the University of Dublin* **(1907)**

Largely as a result of women's activism, Trinity College, Dublin, granted full admission rights to women in 1903. National University, Dublin, and Queens University, Belfast, followed suit six years later. Though, in "The Dead," Molly Ivors would have been able to qualify for a degree (through an examination board) at the same university as Gabriel, she would not have been able to attend classes with him. Their paths, thus, were not as "parallel" as Gabriel perceives them to be.

... In pursuance of the resolutions of the Board of 21st March, 1903, and of the authority granted or confirmed by His Majesty's[1] letter

---

1   *His Majesty's*   Referring to King Edward VII, King of the United Kingdom of Great Britain and Ireland from 1901 to 1910.

of December 1903, women are now admissible to all lectures, examinations, and degrees in arts and the Medical School, but not to fellowships or scholarships. The teaching of men and women in the college is in common, except that a separate anatomical department has been set apart for women in the Medical School. The resolutions … provided in certain cases for lectures being given to women in a separate building outside the college....

D. Literary Contexts

1. from John McCall, *The Life of James Clarence Mangan* (1887)

Joyce admired Irish romantic poet James Clarence Mangan. In this passage of an early biography, young Mangan is described as a "knight-errant" pursuing an "errand" of acquisition "for [the] sake" of a beloved female playmate to whom "he could refuse ... no request." This anecdote may have inspired both the quest in Joyce's "Araby" and the choice to refer to the unnamed object of the protagonist's affection as "Mangan's sister."

... In early issues of the *Irishman* newspaper, ... a series of remarkable papers on the Irish poets appeared, one of which was an epitome of Mangan's early life, a portion of which seemed to be penned by the poet himself....

In illustration of the poet's abstracted and retiring disposition when he was eight years old or so, and while, we suppose, the family resided in their humble lodgings in Chancery-lane, it makes mention of a little girl of curling sunny locks, a couple of Summers his senior, who was his constant playmate in their innocent outdoor sports, to whom he unburthened his childish secrets, with whom he shared his gooseberries and sugar-plums, and who ... soon acquired such a complete sway over the timid boy that he could refuse her no request that she asked—there was no feat, however daring, that he would not attempt to perform for her sake. There was a certain love-ditty most particularly pleasing to her, and it so occurred that one hazy morning, as the pair were playing as usual in one of the open halls adjacent to their abode, they were agreeably surprised by hearing this favourite melody warbled forth by an itinerant ballad-singer, with an admiring auditory round him, as he proceeded at a rather slow pace down the great thoroughfare of Bride-street. After the children had listened for some time in silent admiration the whim seized the exacting young creature to despatch her knight-errant with a small copper in hand to purchase the ballad, and in his anxiety to please he quickly started on his mission, oblivious that he was bareheaded and the rain commencing to fall heavily at the time. Arriving in the centre of the motley crowd, he was still, as usual, so timid and retiring in his nature that he could not find it in his heart to disturb the lusty melodist, or even for one moment interrupt his playmate's favourite song, by making his purchase. The multitude passed up Werburgh-street, and still the entranced Mangan essayed not to fulfil his errand; on through Skinner's-row, High-street, Corn-market, and Cutpurse-row, with a like result; and it was only when the singer and his admirers emerged into the open thoroughfare of Thomas-street that our hatless friend, now feeling himself thoroughly drenched to the skin, bethought of the mission he was sent on, and summoned up courage enough to buy the ballad....

2. from E.Œ. Somerville and Martin Ross, *The Real Charlotte* (1894)

> While *The Real Charlotte* focuses on the Protestant Anglo-Irish aristocracy, *Dubliners* is primarily concerned with the Catholic lower-middle class. Both texts, however, describe turn-of-the-century Dublin. The opening paragraph of Somerville and Ross's novel, excerpted here, introduces the Protestant section of Dublin's north side.

An August Sunday afternoon in the north side of Dublin. Epitome of all that is hot, arid, and empty. Tall brick houses, browbeating each other in gloomy respectability across the white streets; broad pavements, promenaded mainly by the nomadic cat; stifling squares, wherein the infant of unfashionable parentage is taken for the daily baking that is its substitute for the breezes and the press of perambulators on the Bray Esplanade or the Kingstown pier. Few towns are duller out of the season than Dublin, but the dullness of its north side neither waxes nor wanes; it is immutable, unchangeable, fixed as the stars. So at least it appears to the observer whose impressions are only eye-deep, and are derived from the emptiness of the streets, the unvarying dirt of the window panes, and the almost forgotten type of ugliness of the window curtains....

3. Berkeley Campbell, "The Old Watchman," *The Irish Homestead* (2 July 1904)

George Russell (also known as A.E.) sent Joyce this story—which had appeared in Russell's agricultural journal, *The Irish Homestead*—along with a request that Joyce write something similar for the journal.[1] "The Sisters," originally titled "The Old Priest," was Joyce's response. Somewhat modified, "The Sisters" would later become the opening story of *Dubliners*. Though Joyce's story in many ways echoes Campbell's, it denies Russell's request for the type of "pathos" that drives "The Old Watchman." Russell went on to publish "Eveline" and "After the Race" (later included in *Dubliners*), but complaints from *Irish Homestead* readers offended by Joyce's representation of Dublin life compelled Russell to stop with these. It is interesting to consider that an appeal for something "simple, rural," and intended "not to shock the readers" eventually gave rise to *Dubliners*.

When the Electric Tramway Company were laying the lines for their cars some years ago in Dublin, I was a small boy of about twelve, and it used to interest me very much to stand and watch the men at their work.

At that time I used constantly to go to the theatre with my father in the evenings, and we always walked home, as Dad said it was good for us to get a breath of fresh air after coming out of the stuffy theatre, so that we got to know the appearance of the men at work on the line.

There was one old man in particular who took my fancy. He was apparently about sixty-five, and his clean-shaved, wrinkled face had a sad and lonely expression. He was generally employed as the watchman, and we looked out for him each night beside his fire-basket in his little red hut.

Sometimes he was not there, and the hut did not look the same when we did not see him. I called him "my old man," and after he had stopped my hat for me one windy night as it was on the verge of being blown into his fire-basket, I always said "Good-night" to him, and he touched his hat to me just like an old friend. Once when he

---

1 See Appendix B.1.

was established near a crossing, while we were waiting to get through the traffic Dad had quite a conversation with him.

"This is a cold night for that work."

"Yes, sir; yes, sir," and I was very much surprised to hear that he spoke with a very nice accent and a cultivated voice.

"Are you on watch all night, or does someone relieve you?"

"Oh yes, sir! Another chap comes about twelve o'clock to take my place, but I generally stay with him instead of going—ah—home; you see it is lonely here after one or two o'clock."

"But I suppose you are well paid?"

"Oh! it's not too bad, sir. There is your chance of getting over now, sir. Behind that carriage. Watch the young gentleman."

"Here is a shilling for you to get a cup of coffee on your way home tonight."

"No, thank you, sir! I'll not take it; I'll tell you the reason some other time, but I'm very thankful to you all the same for the kind thought."

"Well, well! I suppose you know your own business best; but there's no good in being too proud."

"It's not that, sir. But there aren't many take the trouble of passing a word with the old watchman, and for the sake of old times——! Ah! Some other time, maybe, you would listen to an old man's story."

"I hope so, indeed; are you here every night?"

"Well no, sir, not regularly. I get one or two days a week working on the line, instead of constant night work. And sometimes my cough is too bad for me to get out, and James, that's the other workman, takes it for me. I have had a cough ever since I had pleurisy,[1] and I'm afraid it won't leave me here much longer."

"Oh! it's not as bad as that, I hope. Good night!" said Dad, and I remember the many different conjectures we came to on the way home as to what his story was. Then I got a very bad cold, and was not out with Dad for about a fortnight; but I always asked him when he came in if he had been talking to "my old man"; but he hadn't, and we concluded he had been attacked by his cough again.

When he had not been at his post for a week after I was allowed out, we had nearly given up looking out for him, till one night I saw

---

1   *pleurisy*   Inflammation of tissue surrounding the lungs.

him, and pulled Dad over to talk to him. Dad laughed, and told me not to be in such a hurry, and we made our way over to the corner of the square, although it was not really on our way home, for, as I explained, he would be going further out of our way every night, and we might not get another opportunity.

He looked so pleased to see us, and said he had been in the house with his cough, as we thought.

"Before I begin," said he, "might I ask you, sir, if you are a son of General Culwick's, who used to be commanding at the Royal Barracks[1] twenty or thirty years ago?"

"Yes," said Dad, staring at him, "but how do you come to know anything about him? He has been dead for fifteen years."

"Ah, well! It's all part of my story.

"My father was Dean of St. Patrick's.[2] You are surprised, sir, and you may not believe me. Men in my class of life do not get much credence, but it's God's truth! I was his second son, and was to have gone through Trinity[3] to take my degree and then study for the Bar, but I never got further than my 'Little Go,'[4] although I was four years in college. I was a bad boy—I know it now—and a great anxiety to my poor old father. My eldest brother was a contrast to me in every way; he was hard working, clever and steady, and he got through Sandhurst[5] before he was twenty, and was stationed at the Royal Barracks under your father, sir; and many a time I have dined at the mess there, and at the table with the General, but it was for no good. I only stayed up to the small hours of the morning drinking and gambling, and losing more money than I could ever hope to pay back. To make a long story short, my father called me into his study one morning and told me he had heard of my doings, and spoke very wisely, and offered me a 'start' if I would go to Canada and get away from my bad companions, for he saw I would do no good at home. But I was so hot-headed I flew into a rage and told him I wouldn't take his 'start,'

---

1 *Royal Barracks* British military barracks in Dublin.
2 *St. Patrick's* Cathedral in Dublin.
3 *Trinity* I.e., Trinity College, Dublin.
4 *Little Go* Final freshman examination, taken in a student's second year.
5 *Sandhurst* Common name for Royal Military College, Sandhurst. Located in England, it is where British Army officers were trained.

and that if I was not wanted at home I could find a living for myself. And off I went and never saw my poor father again.

"I need not tell you the life I led in Australia, which was where I went to the goldfields, going from bad to worse, till one day I got a longing to come home, and I lived steady enough till I earned my passage back. That was four years ago now, and I got home, never having heard a word of one of my own people or any of my friends all that time. I landed in Dublin without any recommendations, of course, and you know, sir, how hard it is for a man to give up bad habits. There was not a soul I knew in the old days I could find any trace of, all dead and gone, and I walked past houses I had been a guest in, a disreputable beggar, nothing but strange faces on every side. I have heard since my eldest brother is a General in India. He has kept up the credit of the family and I have let it down. My only sister is dead, and her husband and family live in Fitzwilliam-square.[1] My nephews and nieces! Well, well! It's a funny world, and it's all my own fault. I'll not be here much longer anyhow. One of my pals in Australia (a young doctor who was making a great name for himself, when he took to drink and drifted to the goldfields) told me, many years ago now, that my lungs would never stand a damp climate or exposure to the cold. Well, I suppose I have had a merry life, though not a happy one, and I mustn't be keeping the young gentleman out of his bed so late. It was very kind of you, sir, to listen to me so long, but I had a fancy to tell it to someone before I go! Good night, sir! Ah, no, I don't want any help; I will do very well as I am. Good night, sir!"

And he turned away and we had to come home. However, Dad found out where he lived and had him sent to a hospital, and I used to go and see him very often, but he only lived a few weeks, and I was awfully sorry when he died.

But now I always look at the watchmen on the tram lines and wonder if they have a story like "my old man's!"

---

1   *Fitzwilliam-square*   Square in central Dublin.

OUR WEEKLY STORY.

"THE OLD WATCHMAN."

By BERKELEY CAMPBELL.

When the Electric Tramway Company were laying the lines for their cars some years ago in Dublin, I was a small boy of about twelve, and it used to interest me very much to stand and watch the men at their work.

At that time I used constantly to go to the theatre with my father in the evenings, and we always walked home, as Dad said it was good for us to get a breath of fresh air after coming out of the stuffy theatre, so that we got to know the appearance of the men at work on the line.

There was one old man in particular who took my fancy. He was apparently about sixty-five, and his clean-shaved, wrinkled face had a sad and lonely expression. He was generally employed as the watchman, and we looked out for him each night beside his fire-basket in his little red hut.

Sometimes he was not there, and the hut did not look the same when we did not see him. I called him "my old man," and after he had stopped my hat for me one windy night as it was on the verge of being blown into his fire-basket, I always said "Good-night" to him, and he touched his hat to me just like an old friend. Once when he was established near a crossing, while we were waiting to get through the traffic Dad had quite a conversation with him.

"This is a cold night for that work."

"Yes, sir ; yes, sir," and I was very much surprised to hear that he spoke with a very nice accent and a cultivated voice.

"Are you on watch all night, or does someone relieve you ?"

"Oh yes, sir ! Another chap comes about twelve o'clock to take my place, but I generally stay with him instead of going—ah—home ; you see it is lonely here after one or two o'clock."

"But I suppose you are well paid ?"

"Oh ! it's not too bad, sir. There is your chance of getting over now, sir. Behind that carriage. Watch the young gentleman."

"Here is a shilling for you to get a cup of coffee on your way home to-night."

"No, thank you, sir ! I'll not take it ; I'll tell you the reason some other time, but I'm very thankful to you all the same for the kind thought."

"Well, well ! I suppose you know your own business best ; but there's no good in being too proud."

"It's not that, sir. But there aren't many take the trouble of passing a word with the old watchman, and for the sake of old times —— ! Ah ! Some other time, maybe, you would listen to an old man's story."

"I hope so, indeed ; are you here every night ?"

"Well no, sir, not regularly. I get one or two days a week working on the line, instead of constant night work. And sometimes my cough is too bad for me to get out, and James, that's the other workman, takes it for me. I have had a cough ever since I had pleurisy, and I'm afraid it won't leave me here much longer."

"Oh ! it's not as bad as that, I hope. Good night !" said Dad, and I remember the many different conjectures we came to on the way home as to what his story was. Then I got a very bad cold, and was not out with Dad for about a fortnight ; but I always asked him when he came in if he had been talking to "my old man ;" but he hadn't, and we concluded he had been attacked by his cough again.

When he had not been at his post for a week after I was allowed out, we had nearly given up looking out for him, till one night I saw him, and pulled Dad over to talk to him. Dad laughed, and told me not to be in such a hurry, and we made our way over to the corner of the square, although it was not really on our way home, for, as I explained, he would be going further out of our way every night, and we might not get another opportunity.

He looked so pleased to see us, and said he had been in the house with his cough, as we thought.

"Before I begin," said he, "might I ask you, sir, if you are a son of General Culwick's, who used to be commanding at the Royal Barracks twenty or thirty years ago ?"

"Yes," said Dad, staring at him, "but how do you come to know anything about him ? He has been dead for fifteen years."

"Ah, well ! It's all part of my story."

"My father was Dean of St. Patrick's. You are surprised, sir, and you may not believe me. Men in my class of life do not get much credence, but it's God's truth ! I was his second son, and was to have gone through Trinity to take my degree and then study for the Bar, but I never got further than my 'Little Go,' although I was four years in college. I was a bad boy—I know is now—and a great anxiety to my poor old father. My eldest brother was a contrast to me in every way ; he was hard working, clever and steady, and he got through Sandhurst before he was twenty, and was stationed at the Royal Barracks under your father, sir ; and many a time I have dined at the mess there, and at the table with the General, but it was for no good.

I only stayed up to the small hours of the morning drinking and gambling, and losing more money than I could ever hope to pay back. To make a long story short, my father called me into his study one morning and told me he had heard of my doings, and spoke very wisely, and offered me a 'start' if I would go to Canada and get away from my bad companions, for he saw I would do no good at home. But I was so hot-headed I flew into a rage and told him I wouldn't take his 'start,' and that if I was not wanted at home I could find a living for myself. And off I went and never saw my poor father again.

"I need not tell you the life I led in Australia, which was where I went to the goldfields, going from bad to worse, till one day I got a longing to come home, and I lived steady enough till I earned my passage back. That was four years ago now, and I got home, never having heard a word of one of my own people or any of my friends all that time. I landed in Dublin without any recommendations, of course, and you know, sir, how hard it is for a man to give up bad habits. There was not a soul I knew in the old days I could find any trace of, all dead and gone, and I walked past houses I had been a guest in, a disreputable beggar, nothing but strange faces on every side. I have heard since my eldest brother is a General in India. He has kept up the credit of the family and I have let it down. My only sister is dead, and her husband and family live in Fitzwilliam-square. My nephews and nieces ! Well, well ! It's a funny world, and it's all my own fault. I'll not be here much longer anyhow. One of my pals in Australia (a young doctor who was making a great name for himself, when he took to drink and drifted to the goldfields) told me, many years ago now, that my lungs would never stand a damp climate or exposure to the cold. Well, I suppose I have had a merry life, though not a happy one, and I mustn't be keeping the young gentleman out of his bed so late. It was very kind of you, sir, to listen to me so long, but I had a fancy to tell it to someone before I go ! Good night, sir ! Ah, no, I don't want any help ; I'll do very well as I am. Good night, sir !"

And he turned away and we had to come home. However, Dad found out where he lived and had him sent to a hospital, and I used to go and see him very often, but he only lived a few weeks, and I was awfully sorry when he died.

But now I always look at the watchmen on the tram lines and wonder if they have a story like "my old man's !"

TRAINING FOR DOMESTIC WORK.
Some Suggestions.

At the present time there seems to be a distinct inclination among educated women workers to turn their attention to domestic work. Whether this has been accomplished by the scarcity of other well-paid employments, or by a better knowledge of what is expected in domestic work, it is difficult to say. The inclination, however, is there, and the question remains how it is best to encourage it into action. Five years ago no educated Irish woman would have dreamt of undertaking domestic work. If she did, it was in a very round-about way, and under the vague and unsatisfactory title of "lady-help," "mother's-help," or "nursery-governess ;" certainly not "housemaid," "parlourmaid," "cook," or "scullery-maid."

England has given us a lead in this direction in the establishment of a guild of household dames, and the lead is well worth following. Training homes for educated women have been established all over the country, and the London Employment Bureau has done a great work in giving advice on the different branches of work and in obtaining situations for trained

"DUDBRIDGE"
GAS and OIL ENGINES.

LATEST AND "QUITE THE BEST."

Catalogues free from

TUCK & CO., Ltd., Lr. Abbey Street, DUBLIN.

"The Old Watchman" in *The Irish Homestead*, 2 July 1904.

E. Songs

1. Thomas Moore, "O, Ye Dead" (1808)

Originally composed by Irish poet Thomas Moore as one of his 1808 *Irish Melodies*, this song was arranged by Charles Villiers Stanford in 1894. Joyce's brother Stanislaus heard Stanford's arrangement performed in Dublin in 1905: "It sounded as if the dead were whimpering and jealous of the happiness of the living. My bother liked the idea and asked me to send him the song," which, Stanislaus claimed, provided "the idea for 'The Dead.'"

1.

Oh, ye Dead! oh, ye Dead! whom we know by the light you give
From your cold gleaming eyes, though you move like men who live,
Why leave you thus your graves,
In far off fields and waves,
Where the worm and the sea-bird only know your bed,
To haunt this spot where all
Those eyes that wept your fall,
And the hearts that wailed you, like your own, lie dead?

2.

It is true, it is true, we are shadows cold and wan;
And the fair and the brave whom we loved on earth are gone;
But still thus even in death,
So sweet the living breath
Of the fields and the flowers in our youth we wandered o'er,
That ere, condemned, we go
To freeze 'mid Hecla's[1] snow,
We would taste it a while, and think we live once more!

---

1   *Hecla*   Icelandic volcano, believed in the Middle Ages to be one of the gateways to purgatory.

2. Frederic Clay and W.G. Wills, "I'll Sing Thee Songs of Araby" (1877)

Joyce greatly admired the work of Irish poet Thomas Moore, including his 1817 verse tale *Lalla Rookh*, on which the following popular late-century musical cantata was based. The song resonates with Joyce's "Araby" not only in its evocation of a mystical East and its portrayal of romantic yearning, but also more precisely in the speaker's employment of Orientalism to win the object of his affection.[1]

I'll sing thee songs of Araby
And tales of fair Cashmere,
Wild tales to cheat thee of a sigh
Or charm thee to a tear.
And dreams of delight shall on thee break
And rainbow visions rise,
And all my soul shall strive to wake
Sweet wonder in thine eyes ...
And all my soul shall strive to wake
Sweet wonder in thine eyes.

Through those twin lakes where wonder wakes
My raptured song shall sink
And, as the diver dives for pearls,
Bring tears, bright tears, to their brink.
And dreams of delight shall on thee break
And rainbow visions rise,
And all my soul shall strive to wake
Sweet wonder in thine eyes ...
And all my soul shall strive to wake
Sweet wonder in thine eyes.

---

1 For more on Orientalism, see the introduction, page 12.

F. Reviews

1. from Anonymous, *Times Literary Supplement* (18 June 1914)

Dubliners is a collection of short stories, the scene of which is laid in Dublin. Too comprehensive for the theme, the title is nevertheless typical of a book which purports, we assume, to describe life as it is and yet regards it from one aspect only. The author, Mr. James Joyce, is not concerned with all Dubliners, but almost exclusively with those of them who would be submerged if the tide of material difficulties were to rise a little higher. It is not so much money they lack as the adaptability which attains some measure of success by accepting the world as it is. It is in so far that they are failures that his characters interest Mr. Joyce....

Dubliners may be recommended to the large class of readers to whom the drab makes an appeal, for it is admirably written. Mr. Joyce avoids exaggeration. He leaves the conviction that his people are as he describes them. Shunning the emphatic, Mr. Joyce is less concerned with the episode than with the mood which it suggests....

2. from Anonymous, *Athenaeum* (20 June 1914)

... The fifteen short stories here given under the collective title of *Dubliners* are nothing if not naturalistic.[1] In some ways, indeed, they are unduly so: at least three would have been better buried in oblivion. Life has so much that is beautiful, interesting, educative, amusing, that we do not readily pardon those who insist upon its more sordid and baser aspects. The condemnation is the greater if their skill is of any high degree, since in that case they might use it to better purpose.

Mr. Joyce undoubtedly possesses great skill both of observation and of technique. He has humour.... He has also knowledge of the

---

1   *naturalistic*   Naturalism, a literary movement that emerged in the nineteenth century, is a form of literary realism influenced by Charles Darwin's theory of evolution; naturalistic writers attempted to present a lived, everyday reality and to suggest that human character is shaped by a combination of genetic and environmental influences. Naturalistic works were known to discuss the darker aspects of human life, often with a harshly pessimistic attitude.

beauty of words, of mental landscapes (if we may use such a phrase): the last page of the final story is full evidence thereto. His characterization is exact: speaking with reserve as to the conditions of certain sides of the social life of Dublin, we should say that it is beyond criticism. All of the personages are living realities.

But Mr. Joyce has his own specialized outlook on life—on that life in particular; and here we may, perhaps, find the explanation of much that displeases and that puzzles us. That outlook is evidently sombre: he is struck by certain types, certain scenes, by the dark shadows of a low street or the lurid flare of an ignoble tavern, and he reproduces these in crude, strong sketches scarcely relieved by the least touch of joy or repose. Again, his outlook is self-centred, absorbed in itself rather; he ends his sketch abruptly time after time, satisfied with what he has done, brushing aside any intention of explaining what is set down or supplementing what is omitted.

... "The Dead," far longer than the rest, and tinged with a softer tone of pathos and sympathy, leads us to hope that Mr. Joyce may attempt larger and broader work, in which the necessity of asserting the proportions of life may compel him to enlarge his outlook and eliminate such scenes and details as can only shock, without in any useful way impressing or elevating, the reader....

3. from Ezra Pound, "*Dubliners* and Mr. James Joyce," *The Egoist* (15 July 1914)

... Mr. Joyce's merit, I will not say his chief merit but his most engaging merit, is that he carefully avoids telling you a lot that you don't want to know. He presents his people swiftly and vividly, he does not sentimentalize over them, he does not weave convolutions. He is a realist. He does not believe "life" would be all right if we stopped vivisection[1] or if we instituted a new sort of "economics." He gives the thing as it is. He is not bound by the tiresome convention that any part of life, to be interesting, must be shaped into the conventional form of a "story." Since De Maupassant[2] we have had

---

1 *vivisection* Surgery conducted on living organisms for the purpose of scientific experimentation. Anti-vivisection movements first emerged in the late nineteenth century.

2 *De Maupassant* French writer (1850–93) whose short stories are considered foundational to the genre.

so many people trying to write "stories" and so few people presenting life. Life for the most part does not happen in neat little dia-
grams and nothing is more tiresome than the continual pretence that
it does.

Mr. Joyce's "Araby," for instance, is much better than a "story," it
is a vivid writing.

It is surprising that Mr. Joyce is Irish. One is so tired of the Irish
or "Celtic" imagination[1] (or "phantasy" as I think they now call it)
flopping about. Mr. Joyce does not flop about. He defines. He is not
an institution for the promotion of Irish peasant industries. He ac-
cepts an international standard of prose writing and lives up to it.

He gives us Dublin as it presumably is. He does not descend to
farce. He does not rely upon Dickensian caricature. He gives us
things as they are, not only for Dublin, but for every city. Erase the
local names and a few specifically local allusions, and a few historic
events of the past, and substitute a few different local names, allusions and events, and these stories could be retold of any town.

That is to say, the author is quite capable of dealing with things
about him, and dealing directly, yet these details do not engross him,
he is capable of getting at the universal element beneath them.

The main situations of "Madame Bovary" or of "Doña Perfecta"[2]
do not depend on local colour or upon local detail, that is their
strength. Good writing, good presentation can be specifically local, but it must not depend on locality. Mr. Joyce does not present
"types" but individuals. I mean he deals with common emotions
which run through all races.... I think there is a new phase [of Irish
literature] in the works of Mr. Joyce. He writes as a contemporary of
continental writers. I do not mean that he writes as a faddist, mad
for the last note, he does not imitate Strindberg, for instance, or
Bang.[3] He is not ploughing the underworld for horror. He is not
presenting a macabre subjectivity. He is classic in that he deals with

---

1   *Irish or "Celtic" imagination*   Pound is referring to the Celtic Revival, spearheaded by W.B.
    Yeats.

2   *Madame Bovary*   Classic 1847 novel by French author Gustave Flaubert. It incorporates
    details of everyday life in rural northern France;   *Doña Perfecta*   Classic 1876 novel by
    Spanish writer Benito Pérez Galdós. An imaginary Spanish town is depicted in the novel.

3   *Strindberg*   August Strindberg (1849–1912), a Swedish writer and artist whose work is as-
    sociated with the Naturalist and Expressionist literary movements;   *Bang*   Herman Bang
    (1857–1912), a Danish writer associated with the Naturalist and Impressionist movements.

normal things and with normal people. A committee room, Little Chandler, a nonentity, a boarding house full of clerks—these are his subjects and he treats them all in such a manner that they are worthy subjects of art....

I think that he excels most of the impressionist writers because of his more rigorous selection, because of his exclusion of all unnecessary detail....

Mr. Joyce's more rigorous selection of the presented detail marks him, I think, as belonging to my own generation, that is, to the "nineteen-tens," not to the decade between "the 'nineties" and today. At any rate these stories and the novel now appearing in serial form[1] are such as to win for Mr. Joyce a very definite place among English contemporary prose writers, not merely a place in the "Novels of the Week" column, and our writers of good clear prose are so few that we cannot afford to confuse or to overlook them.

---

1   *novel now ... serial form*   Pound is referring to *A Portrait of the Artist as a Young Man*, which ran from 1914 to 1915 in the *The Egoist*. Pound was a literary editor of *The Egoist*, and *Portrait* was serialized at his suggestion.

from the publisher

A name never says it all, but the word "broadview" expresses a good deal of the philosophy behind our company. We are open to a broad range of academic approaches and political viewpoints. We pay attention to the broad impact book publishing and book printing has in the wider world; we began using recycled stock more than a decade ago, and for some years now we have used 100% recycled paper for most titles. As a Canadian-based company we naturally publish a number of titles with a Canadian emphasis, but our publishing program overall is internationally oriented and broad-ranging. Our individual titles often appeal to a broad readership too; many are of interest as much to general readers as to academics and students.

Founded in 1985, Broadview remains a fully independent company owned by its shareholders—not an imprint or subsidiary of a larger multinational.

If you would like to find out more about Broadview and about the books we publish, please visit us at **www.broadviewpress.com**. And if you'd like to place an order through the site, we'd like to show our appreciation by extending a special discount to you: by entering the code below you will receive a 20% discount on purchases made through the Broadview website.

Discount code: **broadview20%**

Thank you for choosing Broadview.

Please note: this offer applies only to sales of bound books within the United States or Canada.

The interior of this book is printed on 100% recycled paper.

PERMANENT